To Greg & Cheryl,

I hope you enjoy.

Love, Mike

A Milestone Day

by

Charles M. Lockner, Sr.

AuthorHouse™
1663 Liberty Drive, Suite 200
Bloomington, IN 47403
www.authorhouse.com
Phone: 1-800-839-8640

©2009 Charles M. Lockner, Sr.. All rights reserved.

No part of this book may be reproduced, stored in a retrieval system, or transmitted by any means without the written permission of the author.

First published by AuthorHouse 3/5/2009

ISBN: 978-1-4389-4495-1 (sc)
ISBN: 978-1-4389-4496-8 (hc)

Printed in the United States of America
Bloomington, Indiana

This book is printed on acid-free paper.

DEDICATION

I want to dedicate this book to my son, Mike, and to my daughter, April for their consistent and loving support.

Contents

Dedication	v
Acknowledgements	ix
Prologue	xi
Chapter 1: The Trio	1
Chapter 2: Freddy	15
Chapter 3: Deep Impressions	21
Chapter 4: Jacky	37
Chapter 5: Cooling Down	49
Chapter 6: Cary	59
Chapter 7: Heated Situations	65
Chapter 8: Total Calamity	81
Chapter 9: All Downhill From Here	95
Chapter 10: Dream Sharing	107
Chapter 11: The Truth Comes Out	113

Acknowledgements

My thanks to my cousin David Erard for his valuable editing support and positive comments.

Many thanks to my dear friend Michael E. Burbridge, M. Ed., L.P.C. (Youth Development Specialist) for his editing support and for his very supportive letter included on the back cover of this book.

Prologue

THE PAGES OF THIS BOOK are firmly implanted within the years of my own youth. How else could it be? It was truly the best of times in many ways. I was young and life was new, and I was in the very middle of a typical middleclass evolution. The middleclass was gaining financial ground in the postwar period, and status awareness as well. But, things seemed to change more slowly then than they do today.

So much has happened so rapidly in the last few decades that we really need to reflect back to times that were simpler. And that is what this book does. It is best to not forget any of the simpler times. As you progress through life, think back and analyze your own experiences from time to time. It is most important to remember your own span of years and benefit from your own experiences - as well as our characters in the pages to follow.

☙

Cary, the principle character, was born at Christian Hospital in St. Louis, Mo. during the early winter of 1944-45. He lived in what was then a very nice middleclass neighborhood. As for now, one wouldn't walk through the neighborhood without police protection. Frankly, I'd be leery even driving through some areas by car.

World War II was still in progress at that time. It's a given fact, then, that Cary was a pre-baby boomer (by a small margin). For most postwar parents the years immediately following the war were a time for pursuing growth and development....very positive years.

The rest of this prologue, and the pages to follow, describe life in the early years of the pre-baby boomers. It was my early era - my earliest life memories. All of the characters, while fictitious, spring from memories of real people that I have known. A few of the incidents did occur in one form or another. However, the names are not real and incidents have been changed or intermixed to respect individual privacy.

Life then was significantly different than life is today. Each era has it's own magic. It can't be duplicated; it never will be duplicated. You see, that was then, and this is now, and they will never be the same.

My earliest memories are of a neighborhood and a place in time that definitely had a uniqueness all its own. I remember huge oak trees and tons of leaves being raked and burned in the fall. The seasons were marked not only by the smell of burning leaves or by winter snowfalls, but by unique experiences and feelings that are now history.

I remember the last brick-paved street in our neighborhood. I relish the memory of one of the last horse-drawn milk wagons. We used to feed the horse, and grab little chunks of ice from the rear of the wagon. There were numerous local shops - the neighborhood grocery store and drugstore where everyone knew your name. There was also the corner bakery shop that we frequented every Saturday morning, plus the local shoe repair shop, and the local deli shop. Everything was accessible within a one or two block area in this then well-kept residential area.

There were also numerous mobile vendors such as the vegetable vendor yelling "fresh vegetables, fresh tomatoes" - sold from a long open-sided truck. There was even the knife and scissors sharpener who drove some sort of peddle-driven vehicle with all his sharpening tools mounted for street-side use. And finally, the hot-tamale man with a pushcart yelling, "Hot Tamales - Red Hot."

But even more than this, there were numerous insects - katydids by the hundreds that announced the coming of sunset, and thousands of crickets that sang through the night with a chorus that doesn't exist today. There were even the local bats that came from only God knows where. We would throw sticks into the air when they came overhead during the fading summer evenings. They would swoop for the sticks, almost as if they enjoyed playing the game, too. For them it was "morning." For us it was often one of the last activities of a long, warm summer day.

I remember that every summer vacation was anticipated with agonizing weeks of waiting as the days grew longer. Then it was finally here, and there were too many things to do to mention. My brother and I would save our allowance for some weeks or months before the annual school picnic. This would then be matched with an equal amount from our parents. The picnic usually was a day-long affair at either of two popular amusement parks - Chain-of-Rocks or The Highland.

Then came the usual summer organized-activities such as softball, and numerous other school-ground activities. And, of course, there was always swimming. These activities were good for awhile, but the real fun things were things that we did or created with our own imagination.

We loved to climb anything - trees, garages, etc. (no drainpipes!). We would go on scavenger hunts through salvage yards and through alleyways checking cans and ash pits for disposed wheels, ropes, cables pulleys and such. These we would use to build a wooden car, sometimes with a real steering wheel with rope wrapped around the steering column and routed through pulleys to the wheel base. We weren't "The Little Rascals" or the "Dead-End Kids." On the contrary, we were also well equipped with bicycles, and street skates, etc. We took adventuresome trips by bicycle to bordering neighborhoods and distant parks. Also, although we had some softball and baseball equipment, we seemed to get at least as much fun playing bottle-cap ball in the alley. Of course, we couldn't do this too often because it took hundreds of bottle-caps. We could really make a mess out of an alley.

It amazes me that with all of the offbeat and exciting things that we did, I seldom remember anyone in our immediate neighborhood group being seriously injured. Even Freddy, who actually jumped from a second story porch with a home-made parachute and "roman candled" straight to the hard dirt yard below, just walked (actually limped) away from it.

Most of all, I remember the neighborhood kids. We were spread over three schools - the local public school and a Lutheran school (both within a one block walk), and a Catholic school that was a good eight to ten block walk from us. We were a real mixed middleclass bunch.

1
The Trio

It was nearly the end of the summer vacation of 1957. And, as in every past year that could be recalled, Cary and his friends had already run the gamut of the usual organized activities such as softball, swimming, etc. Now was the time for either boredom or adlib, when one had to be inventive or submit to the fact that summer was almost over. It was necessary to keep busy or look forward to nothing but the prospect of another school year. Now that can really be depressing for a 12 1/2 year old boy who is on the verge of so many great things. Well, there were still two glorious weeks left in which to make a memorable summer out of this NOT YET fully spent vacation.

It was an unusually pleasant summer morning. One where just waking up can be a treat. Cary lay there in his first waking moments listening to the chorus of early birds outside his window. There was a gentle breeze delivering the fresh morning air across the room, and there was magic in the air this day. Cary just knew that this day was going to be the start of something very special.

He and two of his buddies were planning to go on an outing together. Not the kind where activities are planned by adults, but an outing full of the prospect of new adventure. The only plans discussed the previous day involved such things as where they would be going and what they should take with them. There were no specifics in regards to activities. They were out for adventure - something or anything that constitutes new and previously un-experienced stimulus for young and eager minds.

Apparently, everyone else in Cary's household was still asleep. That is to say everyone except his brother Sonny who was already encamped on the dock at Fairgrounds lake waiting for the big one to snatch his bait. There was no tying Sonny down since he made the community journal sports section by pulling a six pound large-mouth bass out of the lake using nothing but a bamboo pole for tackle.

Cary and his two friends had decided yesterday that they would each carry a backpack of basic food and necessities, and that they would be going down to the Mississippi river. There were no plans for such things as swimming, or boating etc. No, not at all. This was to be strictly adlib adventure - an explore and conquer attitude was the order of the day. Well, it was now or never, since to lie here any longer was intolerable. After all, it was already 6:30 a.m., not to mention the fact that Cary's bladder was stretched to the limit.

Within 15 minutes Cary was dressed, packed, and had inventoried his backpack. He had all the important items for a days outing -

one can of pork & beans, two semi-hard biscuits from last night's dinner, three Baby Ruth candy-bars, and some powdered Tang orange drink. He then included his pocket-knife (complete with can opener), and a few paper cups carefully protected inside of an empty can. And last, he inserted the centerfold from his brother's Playboy magazine that had been hidden under Sonny's mattress for the past week.

Out the door and down the block to Fred's house he went as fast as a jackrabbit. Freddy was a year older than Cary and Jack, and would probably appreciate the centerfold item. Jack was already sitting in Fred's front yard waiting for Fred to finish what seemed to him like the longest bathroom session on record. Freddy was notorious for spending long periods of time on the toilet. Jacky called it his study.

"Hi, Jack," yelled Cary from the sidewalk. "Where's Freddy?"

"Aw, the great scholar is still in his 'study' (bathroom). I've been waiting for him for 15 minutes already."

Cary laughed as he dropped his backpack to the wet grass beside Jack. Jack was sitting on his backpack to stay dry.

"Hey, Jacky!" said Cary. "Want to see something really cool?"

"Don't tell me; you sneaked your sister's diary from her dresser again. Right? What wimp has she gone ga-ga over this time?"

Jack had bright red hair, and a fair complexion that usually turned various shades of red under stress or when he was embarrassed. He seemed a little pale yet this morning, and still a little sleepy eyed.

"Naw, nothing like that this time," chuckled Cary. "Boy was she angry when I asked her how her lover-boy Tom was fairing. I almost had to admit to her that I'd been reading her life history again. She swore she'd blind me in my sleep with acid if I ever touched her diary again. Besides, she hasn't really written anything exciting since Tommy Foyer tried to unsnap her bra. Hey, Jacky, check this out."

Cary reached into his backpack and pulled out his brother's June centerfold, and handed it to Jack unopened.

"Wow!" exclaimed Jack as he unfolded it with an excited grin on his face. "Where did you get this?" His color improved a little bit, and his eyes were wide open now.

"It's my brother's - next to fishing I think girls are his favorite pass-time."

"Hey, perverts! Whataya got there?" yelled Fred as he closed the screen door. It appeared that Fred was planning a long day judging by the fully stuffed gym bag he was carrying.

"Come and see, oh great scholar." said Jack. "What have you got in the bag, Fred? Look's like your leaving home for good."

By now Fred was right on top of them, and snatched the centerfold out of Jack's hands. "Wow! Super! Say, where's the rest of the magazine?"

Cary laughed and said, "Well, we're not all packrats like you. What have you got in there, anyway? We're only going for the day you know. At least Jack and I plan to come home tonight."

"Oh, my gym bag?" asked Fred Freeman absentmindedly as he eyed the centerfold. "Your brother asked me to bring his fishing boots that I borrowed last week, since we are going right past the lake on our way. The rest is just some sandwiches and my pellet pistol."

Fred's eyes never broke contact with the centerfold - that is until Jack snatched it back again.

"Hey, guy! Be careful with that," said Cary. "I dont want Sonny to know that I took it. You tear it and my ass is mud." Cary snatched the centerfold and tucked it back into his backpack. "Say, Fred. Why don't you put your sandwiches in my backpack and we can take turns carrying it? The boots will be history as soon as we pass Sonny by the lake. Okay?"

And so it went. Fred threw the now empty gym bag back onto his front porch, and they were off. They were a funny looking trio walking down Clay Avenue - skinny Freddy nearly a head taller than either Jack or Cary, and the two little guys carrying the backpacks while Fred cleaned his sunglasses in hopes of a better look at the centerfold.

Fred reached for the backpack on Cary's back.

"Hey, get your hands out of there," squawked Cary. "What are you after, anyway? It's too early to eat, and I'm not getting the centerfold out again - your gonna wear it out."

"I'm gonna tell your brother if you continue to be so tight with HIS property," said Fred.

"Oh yeah!" exclaimed Cary. "Why don't you do your reading in your study later? What do you do in there for so long, anyway - play with yourself?"

Fred gave Cary a playful shove, and they continued towards the park.

Soon they were in Fairgrounds Park and approaching the lake. It was a toss-up whether Sonny would be by the main dock or across the bridge next to the restrooms. Sonny spotted them first, since they were heading east and Jack's red hair stood out like a beacon in the early sunlight.

"Hey, guys! Did you bring my boots with you?" shouted Sonny from almost a city block away. He wedged the handle of his rod into a large knothole in the dock, and was pulling a stringer out of the water when they arrived. He was obviously set on showing off the two catfish that he had already pulled in during his first hour's effort.

"Not bad, Bro!" said Cary. "Gonna use them for bait?"

Sonny just smiled as he set the stringer back into the water and reached for his boots. He was planning on moving down the line to the bank of the lake where the boots might be needed. "Thanks, Fred. Where you guys going first?" He already knew that they were heading to the river in general.

It was Jack who answered, "We're going down to the sewer outlet to look for Fred's morning bowel movement. That ought to kill about 30 minutes from start to finish."

Fred smacked Jack jokingly across the back of his head. Jack didn't acknowledge; he was busy rooting around in Sonny's tackle box.

"What do you do with all this stuff, anyway?" asked Jack. "You've got enough items in here to clean out the lake without a break."

Sonny's tackle had graduated upward since his famous 6 pound large mouth bass catch with a bamboo pole. The journal had paid him $150 for an interview about his catch and fishing history to date. He would have told them his life story for nothing, of course. But it was standard practice to pay the $150 fee for sports related interviews. The tackle box was filled with numerous small accessories in an effort to accommodate his new rod and reel.

About that time something took Sonny's bait, and judging by the bow in his rod it was a rather large prospect. However, this particular fish didn't get to its current size without learning a few tricks of his own, and he was quickly gone - with the bait for his breakfast.

"Did it again!" said Sonny. "I'll get you yet - Its just a matter of time, my friend."

This was probably true, since Sonny seemed to have a relentless pursuit built into his well-developed fishing instincts. Sometimes you would swear that he could see deep into the muddy water where no other human eye could see.

"Well, good fishing Sonny," said Fred. "We gotta go now - important places to go, people to see, and things to do."

Then they were really on their way. About a half hour later they were already as far as O'fallon Park. Another half hour put them down by the riverbank. But the river wasn't really their primary interest. There was a train switching station nearby where they could usually pick up some free (but used) dry cell batteries that had been discarded by the switchmen after their lanterns began to loose some of their intensity. They were still adequate for starting model airplane engines and for powering low voltage lamps in their clubhouse. It was only 8:30, but the heat of the day was already upon them. This was going to be a hot one for sure, even by St. Louis standards.

"Hey Fred!" said Jack. "How far down would you say that water is?"

They were standing on a bluff with at least a twenty-five foot straight drop to a muddy, sloping bank that met the water about five feet outward from the bluff.

Cary spoke before Fred could answer. "I'd say about 30 feet. What do you think, Fred?"

"I'll bet you guys I can piss further-out than either of you," said Jack.

Thus began a brief contest, followed by a five minute break for a candy bar (and two minutes for Freddy to remove his briefs and chuck them into the water). For what it's worth, Fred outdistanced the both of them. But but he accidentally forced a wet fart that cost him his underpants for the day.

Upon arrival at the train switching station they encountered a couple of rather large rats rummaging in one of the trash piles. Now Fred was a little perverted about animals of any kind. He liked to shoot anything that moved, flew, or crawled.

"Quick, Cary - Give me my pellet pistol out of your backpack. I'm gonna get one of 'em." Fred's eyes looked a little wild, and he had a strange grin on his face from ear to ear.

Cary opened the backpack and handed him the pellet pistol. The trash pile was about 40 feet away; so the three of them began to inch a little closer. At a distance of about 25 feet Freddy took a careful bead on the larger of the two rats. And just as Fred was about to shoot the varmint, it stood up on its hind legs and looked right at him. He must have stood almost a foot tall - but only for a few seconds.

Wow, Fred. The suckers looking right at us," whispered Cary.

There was a pop from the pellet pistol, followed by two more in close succession. The first pellet hit the larger rat square in the chest; the second missed completely, but was not needed. The third pellet was intended for the second rat which was already on the run. They thought that Fred winged it, but then it was gone - having found a hole in the trash pile for a quick retreat.

"Hey, boys! What do you think you are doing?" shouted a voice from behind. They whirled to face the duty switchman, believing that they were in big trouble. But there stood a middle-age, slightly graying, pleasant-looking individual with a broad, warm smile on his face.

"We didn't mean no harm, mister." said Jack. "It was only a rat."

The switchman broke into friendly laughter, and said. "That's alright, boys. I've been known to take a few pot-shots at them myself. But, I must warn you that they've got a lot of friends. You'll never get them all."

Cary and jack were smiling now. Fred was still a little shaken by the surprise arrival of the switchman, and was nervously tucking the pellet pistol into the backpack when he accidentally discharged another pellet with a louder than normal - POW!

"Whoa!" screamed Cary, since the backpack was still on his back. "Whataya tryin' to do, Fred - shoot my rear-end off?"

Jack was almost hysterical over this incident, but suppressed his laughter because of the switchman - whose reaction was still to be seen.

"Are you okay, son?" asked the switchman with genuine concern for Cary. "Boy," he said to Fred, "Didn't anybody ever teach you what a safety is for?"

"Ah..ah, yes sir," mumbled Fred as he applied the safety and once again tried to place the pistol into the backpack. But Cary was removing the backpack from his back to assess the damage. Jack was bright red by this time from trying to suppress his now nearly uncontrollable laughter. Cary reached into the backpack, and could feel something gooey inside. He extracted the gooey cylinder, which turned out to be a wounded can of pork-n-beans.

Now everyone was laughing - including Fred (half because of relief that he hadn't damaged anything of permanent value).

Cary reached into the pack again, and this time he extracted a wounded sandwich with a quarter-inch hole right through the center. Apparently the pellet had gone through the sandwich first, and had then penetrated the can of beans. No one gave any thought to the longer-term significance of only one hole existing in the can.

"Well, Dead-eye," said Cary, "it looks like another stunt like that one and you'll be eating that rat for your lunch."

This would have added to the humor, but the switchman had turned rather serious. A truck had just swung onto the narrow dirt road about 200 yards down, and was heading their way.

"That'll be my boss, boys. We'd better walk away from the dead rat before he gets here. He might not take too friendly at your target practice on company property," said the switchman. "What are you boys doing down here besides shooting rats?"

Cary was tying a handkerchief around his wounded beans, and placing them back inside the backpack, hole-side upward. Fred quickly placed the pellet pistol back into the backpack.

"We were hoping to find some used dry cells here, sir," said Fred. "We use'em for our clubhouse lights and things."

The truck was almost upon them, and the switchman said, "Come on, boys. I've got three or four used ones inside the shack that you can have. My name's Jerry, by the way. What's yours?"

Cary responded first, followed by Jack. Fred answered, too, although his name had already come out in the aftermath of the pork-n-bean slaying.

The truck pulled up in front of the shack just as they reached the door. The man driving was younger than the switchman, but not nearly as friendly looking. He handed Jerry a schedule of train routings. Then he waved a quick goodbye, and told Jerry to see that the kids were off the property post-haste. Jerry just nodded an acknowledgement, and told him that he was going to give us some used batteries and send us on our way.

The truck was out of sight by the time the boys had said their good byes and thanks before heading on their way. As they passed the trash pile, Fred broke away and ran over to the dead rat. He picked it up by the tail and did a thorough examination of his kill. Then he whirled it over his head three times and slung it into the nearby trees. Then Fred rejoined them again with a weird smile on his face, and they were on their way.

Freddy is a strange dude, thought Cary.

2
Freddy

Freddy was a bit unusual, to say the least. Aside from the fact that he liked to play with water bugs, and liked to throw rocks at anything that moved (in the air or on the ground), he hadn't been to school for most of the last two years. He had always had trouble academically. But his problems peaked the year before last early in the first semester. There was a rather vivid scuffle with a former school chum that ended with Freddy getting the worst part of the deal. The next day Fred showed up with an ice pick in his boot. It's hard to know exactly what was going through his mind, but one thing is certain. His already badly damaged ego and low self-esteem were at a new all-time low. He was psychologically injured, and wasn't in the mood to take anymore humiliation or ridicule on this day. Maybe the ice pick was just insurance against his damaged ego. I really think that, other than the security that it provided him psychologically, nothing more would have happened....that is, if Johnny Tempen hadn't already decided to carry things just a bit further than he had yesterday. Such was Johnny's nature and his reputation as the class bully.

Johnny had smirked at Fred in class several times when he saw Fred looking at him. Then during morning recess, Johnny couldn't leave well enough alone. Fred was keeping well to himself today, and was simply sitting on one of the benches placed under one of the larger school yard oak trees. Everything else in the school yard was brick, except for the areas surrounding the few trees that had been left in place for their shade and aesthetic value.

Johnny approached Fred from the other side of the tree. He leaned around the tree trunk and whispered into Freddy's ear, "How's the chicken shit punk's temper today?"

Freddy was startled, and about a quart of adrenaline was released into his system immediately. He turned with a start and looked right at Johnny's pimpled face. Johnny just grinned and spit a glob of mucous that landed on Fred's right cheek. Then seeing Fred's combined look of fear, hate, and furious anger, Johnny simply laughed as he turned to run.

Freddy screamed a wild scream and wiped the spit off his cheek with his left sleeve. Without even consciously being aware of it, he had also gone to a stooped position and grasped the handle of the ice pick that was in his right boot. Johnny was about six feet away when Fred stood full upright with the ice pick in his hand. Johnny was about ten feet away by the time Fred had grasped the ice pick by the pointed end. He was about fifteen feet away when Freddy furiously flung the pick towards Johnny, and it stuck firmly underneath the right shoulder blade.

Johnny seemed to halt on a dime, screamed a ghastly high-pitched scream, and fell forward to the ground, just as Freddy was upon him. Fred landed on top of Johnny's buttocks and, ignoring the ice pick completely, grasped Johnny by the hair and began slamming Johnny's face into the schoolyard's brick-covered surface.

Johnny's frantic screams finally brought Fred back to his senses. He released Johnny's hair and stood up. Then he looked around to see if anyone had seen what he had done. By this time several students had stopped their play, and at least a dozen students with startled looks were watching Fred and Johnny at close range.

There was poor Johnny with an ice pick sunk about an inch and a half into his back, lying on his stomach with his head raised sideways, and blood just streaming from his nose in spurts. He was half supporting himself with his left arm, but his right arm hung limply by his side. The most audible sound for just a few seconds was Johnny's awful sobs of shock and confusion.

Then Freddy found his tongue, and began saying (first softly, as if to himself; and then in increasing volume), "I didn't mean to do it! I didn't mean TO DO IT! I DIDN'T MEAN TO DO IT!!!" Then he, too, started to cry in great sobs.

About this time, Mr. Minsky, the schoolyard monitor for today arrived at the scene.

"Oh my God!" cried Mr. Minsky. He seemed to turn pale for a second, and staggered back a pace or two. When he regained his composure he approached Johnny and stooped to Johnny's side.

Another teacher was running across the schoolyard when Mr. Minsky shouted back to her to call an ambulance. She continued to run closer until she was about ten feet away. Then she stopped abruptly, put her hand over her mouth and gasped.

Mr. Minsky repeated in a slightly milder tone, "Call an ambulance." And she turned and ran toward the school building.

By this time Freddy was speechless. He had two fingers in his mouth, and he was actually drooling down his chin and crying at the same time. Johnny was just lying there now and moaning, and his body would quiver all over convulsively every several seconds. He was going into shock. Both Fred and Johnny were white as sheets, each for his own reasons.

Fred, in spite of barrages of questions, resorted to becoming a mute for the rest of the morning until his father came to pick him up from school at noon. Fortunately for Freddy, no one had actually seen him throw the ice pick - least of all, Johnny, who was on the run and laughing at the time. Nor did anyone know how it started, and Fred wasn't saying a word. The school board expelled Fred pending investigation, but there was insufficient evidence to substantiate legal proceedings. Fred was enrolled three weeks later in the local Lutheran school a few blocks away. However, his attendance thereafter was intermittent at best, and his grade average fluctuated between D and F.

Johnny Tempen recovered very quickly, since none of his injuries were very serious. He required a tetanus shot, some antibiotics, and minor wound surgery for cleaning purposes. He missed two days of school with his nose packed with cotton. It's rumored that upon his return Johnny wasn't nearly the former bully that he had been before the ice pick incident.

Good for Freddy. I never did like bullies. They seem to snuff the life out of so many things, especially some of the more timid, young, impressive minds around them.

3
Deep Impressions

Cary, Fred, and Jack were backtracking along the railroad tracks toward the point where they had first come to the river this morning. They were keeping their eyes open for miniature discarded alcoholic beverage bottles - the little single-serving bottles used to serve paying passengers who purchased a drink in route on the passenger trains. They were becoming increasingly difficult to find since the airlines had succeeded in taking a considerable percentage of the passenger travel during the last decade. But that made them all the more desirable as a collector's item from the boys' point of view.

Jack shouted, "I see one!" and ran ahead about ten feet to retrieve a discarded Jim Beam bottle.

Fred asked, "Is it empty?"

Cary laughed and asked Fred, "Why does it matter? You wouldn't drink out of one of those, would you?"

Fred didn't comment, and the three of them continued along the tracks at a slow pace. It wasn't very long before they were back to the bluff that had been the scene of their contest about an hour and a half ago. The two backpacks were getting heavy with the batteries that they had gotten from the switchman. So they decided to take another break under a large and very old oak tree that was growing right at the edge of the 25 foot bluff that they had passed earlier.

"Hey Fred," said Cary. "Help me get this thing off my back. I'm getting a cramp in my shoulder. It's your turn to carry this thing anyway."

Fred assisted Cary while Jack eased his backpack to the ground, and started to root for some goodies for a snack. A welcome breeze came out of nowhere and continued to blow intermittently while they were settling down. They took turns emptying Jack's canteen, and Jack kicked off his heavy boots to let his feet enjoy a little bit of the intermittent breeze. The morning moisture had lifted some time ago, and the day was getting progressively hotter.

"Are you guys getting hungry yet?" asked Jack as he rubbed his stomach. "The candy bar I ate earlier didn't last long at all."

Cary replied, "Hey, lets have some 'real' food. More junk food will only make me queasy."

So the three of them settled down in the shade of the old oak tree, and proceeded to see what they had between them. Jack pulled out an apple and two bananas. Cary dug out the wounded can of pork & beans and the two half-stale biscuits that he had packed earlier. A tug boat was working it's way up the river pushing three large barges. The pilot apparently saw them and blew his whistle, and they replied with an excited waving of hands.

"Want a biscuit, Fred?" asked Cary.

Fred replied, "No, I think I'll have one of those peanut butter sandwiches that I brought, and maybe some beans. Cary passed the leaky can of beans to Fred. Fred looked puzzled for a moment, then asked, "How are we going to open this thing? Or are we supposed to just suck the juice out from the pellet hole in the side of the can?"

Jack chuckled as Cary just reached into his backpack and pulled out his pocket knife complete with can opener.

"Well, Freddy," said Cary smilingly, "You can use this, or you can just take the pellet pistol and shoot the thing completely to pieces, since you already had a good start earlier."

Fred snickered a little bit, but was obviously a little bit embarrassed by his recollection of the earlier accidental discharge of the pellet pistol. In one shot he had wounded the sandwich that he now held in his hand, as well as the can of beans.

Jack was now flushed red with the humor of the situation as he added, "Fred wants to make sure that everything he eats is dead first."

Within a few minutes Fred had the can of pork and beans opened, and Cary was busy pouring some water from his canteen into three paper cups. To each cup he added a generous portion of Tang, and began stirring them with the blade of his pocket knife.

"Hey! What are we supposed to eat the beans with, anyway?" asked Fred.

Cary reached into his backpack and pulled out two more paper cups. "Here, use these."

Fred poured a portion of the beans into each of the two cups, and kept the largest portion inside the can for himself. And so they began to enjoy their small banquet. Cary shook some of the beans from his paper cup into his mouth, and took a bite of stale biscuit. Jack went to work on one of the bananas, while Fred, using his own pocket knife, began loosening the remaining beans from the bottom of the can.

"Hey, Jacky! I thought you weren't supposed to have bananas," said Cary.

"Why is that?" asked Fred.

"His mother says he has fits when he eats bananas," answered Cary (somewhat jokingly with a smile).

Jack showed a severe frown of resentment, and exclaimed that that wasn't true.

"Yes it is, Jack." replied Cary, still smiling. "I heard your mother telling my mom that once you ate too much banana pudding and practically had a seizure when she made you take a bath."

"Do you believe everything you hear, Cary?" asked Jack indignantly. "Maybe I just don't like taking baths."

Cary gave Jack a serious glance, but said nothing in reply. He had just realized from Jack's indignity that it was probably a true story, and maybe Jack did have seizures.

Fred was chuckling at all of this. And at the same time he was shaking the last of the beans from the upraised can directly into his mouth. All of a sudden Fred stopped, seemed to gag, and dropped the can of beans to the ground. He grasped his throat and made choking sounds.

At this Jack really became indignant, since he was certain that Fred was doing a mock act of someone having a seizure, and he was the object of the joke.

Jack jumped to his feet, dropped his empty banana peel, and shouted at Fred, "Cut it out, Freddy! That's not funny, and I don't have seizures. And even if I did, they don't happen like that anyway."

Cary now knew for certain that Jack did, indeed, have seizures. Otherwise, how would he know so much about them? But none of this stopped Fred, even when Jack kicked dirt on him with one of his sock clad feet.

"Cut it out, Fred, or I'm really going to kick you."

"Wait a minute, Jack," said Cary excitedly as he, too, jumped to his feet and dropped his cup of beans. "I think he's really choking."

By this time Fred was standing. He seemed to be a bright red as he strained and gave a loud hacking cough. From out of Fred's mouth came a few crushed beans, some bile from his stomach, and one small foreign object. Then, still bending over, he gasped and drew in a huge breath of fresh air. He cleared his throat with an awesome sound, and spit. Still bent over and with tears coming from his eyes he asked in bewilderment, "What was that?"

Jack and Cary both looked to the ground, and there in the midst of a little pool of beans and bile was a little, grey bead. It came together for both of them simultaneously. They looked at each other, then at Fred, and then back at each other again, and broke into simultaneous laughter.

Fred looked at the two of them in amazement at first. He thought, I nearly died, and they're laughing. Then the irony of it hit him, too, and he began to laugh with them. He had nearly choked to death on the pellet that was inside of the wounded can of beans. It had been there, of course, ever since Fred had accidentally discharged the pellet pistol back at the switching station. *Better in the can of beans than in my back,* thought Cary.

All three of them had forgotten about Jack's indignation, and gave no more conscious attention to that issue for the present time.

Fred was still breathing a bit heavily, but he was also chuckling in between breaths. Cary and Jack were still really laughing when Fred said, "Cool it, guys. I need to catch my breath."

They gradually became more sympathetic to Fred's experience, and Jack began to pat Fred on the back since he was still coughing a little. But Fred brushed Jack's arm away, and mumbled something like it wasn't helping him at all.

Well, things finally settled down after a few minutes, and the three of them were back in sitting positions. But they sat several feet away from where they were before in order to get farther away from Fred's beans and barf. They had moved over to the edge of the bluff, and finished the remnants of their meal with their feet dangling over the edge. The breeze had now stopped, and the day was becoming very hot and dry, except for the humidity that was coming off the river. They each had two more cups of Tang orange drink. It actually tasted quite tart because the water from Cary's canteen had become very warm.

"Say, Fred!" said Jack casually.

"That's my name, don't wear it out," answered Fred.

"I'll bet I can out-distance you now," replied Jack, referring to their earlier pissing contest.

"Your on!" exclaimed Fred, and quickly jumped to his feet.

Cary got up very slowly and stretched, and Fred stood right by the edge of the bluff looking straight downward. It was a good 25 foot drop to the small stretch of muddy land below them that met the river about five or six feet outward from the bottom of the bluff.

Jack chuckled and asked, "No rules?"

Fred gave him a strange look, and said, "Fine! What have you got up your sleeve?"

Jack didn't bother to put on his boots. He simply turned and headed for the large oak tree, and began to climb the trunk. A few feet out of hand's reach from the ground was a large branch that stretched at least twenty-five feet straight outward over the river. Jack quickly succeeded in reaching this branch, and began to work his way out onto the limb by using a higher branch for a grip to balance himself.

Cary, who was standing several feet back from the edge of the bluff, started to chuckle at the thought that Jacky would go to this extreme to win a meaningless contest. Then it occurred to him that, although the limb was only about seven feet above the bluff on which they were standing, it was probably better than 30 feet above the lower ground and the water level.

"Hey, Jacky! You better hold tight 'cause its a long way down," said Cary.

Jacky, who was already about eight feet out onto the limb, stopped and looked down. The view from there shook him up a little bit.

But then he remembered the time that he had dared Cary to climb a scaffold to the top of their school building (four stories up) to fetch an egg out of a bird's nest. And Cary had done it. So Jacky simply said, "No sweat!" and continued outward onto the furthest part of the limb that he dared to chance.

None of them had given any thought to the fact that this rather large branch also looked rather barren of leaves. As a matter of fact, it looked very, very dead and brittle.

Fred was waiting for Jack to get positioned, and he was still determined to follow through with the contest. But he was much more interested in Jack's daring feat than in actually winning the contest (which he stood no chance of winning under these circumstances anyway).

"Ready, Jack?" asked Fred, since Jack had stopped after advancing about twelve feet outward onto the limb.

Jack looked over his shoulder with a sheepish grin, and said, "Ready!" And just as he reached down to unzip his pants with his right hand, the limb beneath his feet yielded a gut-wrenching, loud cra-a-ack! Jack's grip on the upper limb with his left hand was useless now since the upper limb had dwindled to only an inch or so in thickness at this distance outward. Jack let out a horrible scream as he felt the limb beneath him begin to drop very quickly. He lost his grip on the upper limb, and dropped his whole body to the larger limb beneath him as both he and the outward end of the limb disappeared from Cary's sight. This was immediately followed by a noise that sounded like "sploo-oo-p!"

Cary ran to the edge of the bluff so fast that Fred had to help him catch his balance. Otherwise he would have followed the same fate as Jacky. They both looked downward over the edge of the bluff. And there at the bottom of the bluff was Jack. He was imbedded up to his thighs in the mud about two feet from the water's edge. The end of the broken limb still dangled about five feet over his head, the larger end still loosely attached to the tree trunk by the remaining strands of softer wood. One must marvel at how the Good Lord protects us in our childhood! What could have been disastrous and even fatal (perhaps should have been by the normal laws of nature) had turned out to be only frightening and inconvenient for Jack (and very, very funny in retrospect). Jacky was visibly shaken and embarrassed. But, aside from being thoroughly stuck in the mud, he seemed to be okay.

Cary said, "Jeeze, Jack! What do you do for an encore? Are you okay?"

Fred, who was close enough to the edge to see the whole incident when the limb broke, was emotionally recovered before Jack or Cary. He walked over a few feet to the right until he was straight over Jack, and asked, "Is it okay if I pee now?"

Jacky, who could have urinated in his pants by now, simply looked up at Fred and said, "You may as well, Fred, cause I think I already did."

Cary began to laugh aloud now, with both genuine relief and humor over the outcome of his daring feat.

Apparently, when the limb had broken, it swung downward and inward at a rate which had allowed Jack time to purchase a firm grasp on the narrowing end of the limb. Then, as Jack saw the bluff approaching him at a faster rate than the ground (because of the inward swing of the branch), he had released the limb before the limb struck the bluff. His timing, purely by accident and the grace of God, had targeted him for a drop to the muddiest part of the bank below just a couple of feet from the water. The huge limb was still hanging on by a few fibers.

"I can't move my legs," said Jacky in frustration as he fought to free himself from the mud. He reached upward toward the dangling limb, but the end was a couple of feet above his reach. Then he scratched his head, thereby smearing mud from his hand into his flaming red crop of hair. By this time his complexion was beet red with embarrassment and frustration, and he was becoming increasingly confused.

Cary and Fred watched his futile efforts for a few minutes. Then Fred said, "I think he's trying to reach the end of the limb?"

Cary chuckled and replied in a voice loud enough for Jack to hear, "We may have to feed him until he grows a little more."

"Come on, guys! Think of something. How am I going to get out of here?"

"Say, Jacky! Can I have your baseball card collection?" asked Fred. "I'll trade you for a rope; may even tie the other end to the tree trunk for you."

Cary laughed at Fred's little joke, but he was also becoming aware that Jack was becoming a little panicky. He seemed to still be sinking a little - slowly, but surely. He was now almost up to his groin in thick mud.

"Hey, Fred," Said Cary in a much lower voice. "You better lay off the jokes - he's still sinking."

Fred looked at Cary intently, then back down at Jack, and back to Cary. "You think so?" he asked in alarm.

"Get me out of he-e-e-r-re!" screamed Jacky. He was obviously panicking now. "I think I'm still sinking."

Cary stood up and looked at the big oak tree just three feet to his left. The broken limb was still only loosely attached to the tree trunk. He looked back at Fred, who seemed to have the same idea dawning in his mind too.

Without a word they both went over to the large limb and began to rock it back and forth. It was quite heavy to move at first, being about six inches thick at the base. But it gradually began to swing, and with each swing you could hear more wood cracking.

Jack, who was watching from his mud hole, became encouraged a little. "That's it, guys. Swing that baby. No-no-wait! Don't swing it over my head; that thing looks pretty heavy."

The limb made one more swing past Jack's position, and gave out a loud ripping sound as it plummeted the remaining five feet to the ground about two feet from Jack. It dropped fast enough to imbed the smaller end about three feet into the muddy bank. It hadn't broken away clean though, but had stripped the tree of its bark and wood fiber for a few feet downward along the trunk before snapping away. When it snapped free from the trunk the larger, uppermost part of the limb sprang outward away from the top of the bluff. Only Cary's quick action in grabbing onto the stripped strands of wood fiber saved the limb from being lost to the river. And only Fred's quick response in grabbing onto the waist of Cary's jeans saved Cary from being pulled over the side with the limb. Fred pulled on Cary's jeans, as Cary held onto the wood strands. The outward momentum of the limb yielded to their combined efforts and it came crashing back into the side of the bluff with the large end resting almost even with the top of the bluff.

"Gee, guys!" exclaimed Jack. "What do YOU do for an encore?"

"Oh, Wow!" said Cary. "I thought it was gone."

"Thought IT was gone? We almost lost you with it," replied Fred.

"Well your still gonna loose ME if I don't stop sinking," cried Jack, who was already struggling to get a firmer grasp on the end of the limb. "Hold onto the top of the limb."

Jack grabbed the limb one hand over the other while Fred and Cary steadied the top end of the limb. At first he seemed to make very little progress, wriggling his body while he barely managed one hand just over the other for several grasps. Then he gave a hard pull and freed his left leg. A few seconds later his right leg was free, and he was able to pull himself upward enough to wrap his legs around the limb. He rested a few minutes, panting hard, before proceeding up the tree limb. Then he pulled and shinnied upward until he was just a few feet from the top of the bluff. For every two feet upward he would slide a foot downward.

"Come on, Jacky. Your almost there," encouraged Cary.

Fred reached downward with nearly half his body hanging over the edge while Cary held onto his legs.

"Gotcha, Jacky!" said Fred as he clasped Jack's right hand firmly. And after several seconds of hard effort, Jack was pulled back over the top of the bluff to safe ground. Jack just sprawled there for several minutes catching his breath. Fred did the same.

Cary, who was now sitting a few feet away, saw that Jack only had one sock left. It was then that he realized that they may never have gotten Jack out by themselves if he had been wearing his boots when he fell. His boots were J.C. Penney boondockers - quite in style then, and great for hiking. But they were heavy boots with a broad-based sole, and could not be removed without unlacing them.

"Gee, Jack! Your a mess," said Fred finally. "What are we gonna do with you?"

"I think we should throw him back in, but a little further out so he can take a bath," replied Cary.

Jack looked down at his feet, and saw what a mess he was. His fly was halfway down, and mud was inside of his jeans as well. Actually, by now he was pretty muddy all over. Then the three of them looked over the edge again at the two deep holes and the muddy mess where Jacky had been. Cary looked further down the riverfront and could see where the bluff gradually leveled off to the water line. This, of course, would be their very next stop. This is where they would "clean up their act," or at least Jack, before heading any further.

If moms and dads only knew what troubles and difficulties three young boys could encounter in the course of a day! Actually, it was only approaching noon. And the day was so hot and dry by now that the thick mud had already begun to dry on (and inside of) Jacky's pants. They had better get him down to the level ground for a bath in the river soon, or they might have the equivalent of the rust-frozen tin man in the "Wizard of Oz."

4
Jacky

*F*red, Cary, and Jack were in route to the lower river bank where they would have access to clean up Jack before he became baked with caked mud. Cary and Fred were carrying the backpacks, and Jack was carrying his boots (the only clean, dry item he had left). Jack's thoughts began to drift back to an incident that took place last summer.

It was about three o'clock during a rather hot August afternoon during the summer of 1956. Jack's mother looked out the front door to call Jacky in for a bath.

"Jacki-e-e-e! Jacky, where are you?" yelled Mrs. Green. "Jack! Its time to come in now."

"Where is that boy?" mumbled Mrs. Green to herself, as she closed the screen door and headed for the back kitchen window to check the back yard.

About that time Jack came running around the corner, obviously in great haste. He stole a quick glance over his shoulder just before he cleared the corner. He never broke speed even a little bit, but kept on running and laughing as he ran. Just a few feet behind him was Fred Freeman running as fast as he could in pursuit of Jack. Jacky rounded the hedges bordering their front lawn and headed for the front porch screen door, with Fred no more than four feet behind him. He reached the screen door, opened it, slammed it in Fred's face, and latched it just as Fred reached the door. Fred had to put both hands out to catch the door frame in order to keep from running right through the screen door.

Fred was stunned. He never could figure out how Jack did this, and with such assurance that he would not be caught. It wasn't the first time that Fred had chased Jacky to his front door just in time to have the screen door slammed and locked before Fred could place a hand on him.

"Jack, I swear that the next time you spit on me I'll catch you and make you eat dirt", said Fred in frustration.

Jack just laughed again, and said sarcastically, "Gee, thanks for walking me home, Fred." He was closing the front door as Fred tried in vain to spit through the screen door. Then Fred shook his head, and turned to walk down the porch steps. He would never admit it to Jack, but he was smiling a little bit now. Actually, they had been having a pretty good day, and he had enjoyed the chase enough to make being spit upon almost worth it. But he would have enjoyed the whole episode a lot more if he could have caught Jacky before he had made his almost magical screen door entrance. Just once he would like to see Jack yank on that screen door and find that it was hooked from the inside; then he'd have him for certain. *The wise little jerk*, thought Fred. But, once again, he had to admire Jacky for his nerve and his speed. Fred was taller and lankier than Jack, even last year when this incident had taken place. Because of his longer legs it always took Fred longer to get up to speed than Jack, but he'd catch him someday.

"Jack-i-e-e! Is that you?" asked Mrs. Green from the kitchen.

"Yeah, Mom. Am I home on time?" replied Jack.

"Yes, but get your little buns in here right now. You've got to get a bath before we go to the market. You're not going anywhere with me looking and smelling like something the cat dragged in."

By this time Jack was already in the kitchen, and was reaching for a banana from the basket of fruit that his mother almost always kept on the kitchen table. Jacky really liked bananas, especially when they were overly ripe and a little mushy.

"Get your hand out of that basket!" exclaimed Mrs. Green as she lightly slapped Jack's hand.

"Mom, I've only had one today," replied Jack.

"No, you've had two - one in your breakfast cereal, and one just after lunch."

"Well, how long will it be until we eat again?" asked Jack pleadingly. "I'm hungry now."

Mrs. Green looked at her watch, and then at Jack's pleading eyes underneath that thick red crop of mussed hair, and said, "Well, alright; go ahead. We probably will be eating a little late tonight at the rate we are going. Its going to take awhile to shop today."

Jack had only heard the first part of this. He already had the peeling stripped down and a big bite in his mouth before she even finished speaking. His mother motioned for him to sit down on one of the kitchen chairs, and she began to take off his shoes and socks.

Jack's white socks were almost dark mottled grey already. Fred and Jack had been up to the local auto junkyard a couple of blocks away looking for a steering wheel for a wooden car that they were building in Fred's backyard. On the way back they had been into more than one trashcan looking for other accessories. So far they had four wheels complete with axles from a discarded baby buggy. The also had plenty of junk wood, nails, pulleys, and various small accessories from Fred's dad's tool bench. And they had a heavy-duty wooden handle from an old shovel to use for a steering column. They had dropped the parts in Fred's backyard and exited into the alley. Jack had tripped on one of the alleyway bricks, and Fred called him a clumsy clown. Jack got to his feet (still smiling) and spit on Fred's T-shirt. That had started the chase - down the alley to Clay avenue, up Clay to Lexington, and around the corner to Jack's house.

Last summer they had made a car with a pivoting front wheelbase that you could guide with your feet. But this year they wanted a steering wheel. With rope wound around the steering column and threaded through some pulleys, they could have the closest thing to real steering that they could design in their young imaginations.

"My goodness, Jacky!" she remarked. "How do you manage to get so dirty in just a few hours?"

"I dunno, Mom," mumbled Jack - still eating his third banana for the day.

"Well come on, hon. Let's get you into the tub. Time's a'wastin'. We don't have all day."

Jack headed for the bathroom where he knew his mother had already run his bath water for him. He threw the empty banana peel into the garbage can, and removed the remainder of his clothing on his way into the bathroom, leaving a trail of clothing behind him all the way to the tub. His mother just followed behind, kicking his clothes into a pile outside the bathroom door.

Jack stepped into the tub and remarked with a shiver, "It's cold, Mom."

"Well, we can fix that right now. You just stand there for a minute; I've got more hot water on the stove," said Mrs. Green on her way back to the kitchen stove. Not everyone in the neighborhood had heated water yet. Jack's dad liked to brag about how much money he made, but they didn't seem to live any better than anyone else in the neighborhood. Actually, Jack's dad (and his older brother) went through most of their "spending money" on hunting and fishing trips - where they had been known to drink a lot of beer as well.

She was on the way back into the bathroom, which was just off the kitchen when she said, "Now stand back while I pour."

Unfortunately, his mother tripped on Jack's clothes that she had kicked into a pile just outside the bathroom door, and came into the bathroom with a stumble that almost sent her into the tub with Jacky. She caught her balance, but not in time to prevent spilling most of the pot of hot water right down poor little Jack's chest, stomach, legs, and etc.

"Y-i-i-i-e-e-e-!" yelled Jack as he squinted his eyes in sudden shock and pain.

"Oh my God!" screamed Mrs. Green as she dropped the remainder of the pot of water into the tub - pot and all.

Jack was already crying, but his mother moved very quickly now. She flung the now empty floating pot out of the tub, and it hit the wall with a bong before it dropped to the linoleum covered floor. At the same time she grabbed Jack and pushed him face forward down into the tub of water.

Jacky hit the slanted end of the tub facing forward and slid into the still cooler tub of water (right at the tail-end of another blood-curdling scream). Unfortunately for Jacky, this left him with absolutely no air in his lungs when his head and face followed his sliding body into the water. His mother grabbed for his thick crop of red hair and pulled his face up above the water line, but not before Jack had begun to take another breath.

"Oh, darling!" she exclaimed. "I'm so sorry."

She had Jack sitting up by this point, but he was hacking and coughing so much that his face was beet red, not to mention his chest and stomach, and his "etc." (from the hot water). Jack coughed three more deep coughs and then stopped. He looked up at his mother in disbelief, and then started to cry bitter tears.

"Oh, darling!" she exclaimed again. "Are you alright?"

Of course he wasn't. However, the burner under the pot of water had been turned off for nearly fifteen minutes prior to this regrettable accident. Because of this fact, and because of his mother's quick thinking in quickly dunking him into the much cooler bath water, he really wasn't badly burned. But he was very shaken. His facial color was returning to nearly normal now, but his lips looked strangely blue.

"Oh dear; what have I done? I'm so sorry, darling. I must have tripped on your clothes."

His mother looked behind her, and saw that Jack's shirt had hung-up on the bathroom door hinge. Apparently she had snagged her foot in one of the sleeves, and the shirt had nearly ripped into two pieces.

Finally Jack spoke. "Ye-ye-yes," he had difficulty in saying through his tears. "I'm okay, Mom." He sniffled twice, and continued with, "Are you okay, Mom?"

She was relieved for the moment, and replied that she was fine. Actually, she had twisted her ankle somewhat, and had banged her thigh on the edge of the tub, too. But she was only now becoming aware of her own pains.

Jack's lips were still very blue, and his eyes looked funny.

"Are you sure you're okay, honey?" she asked him again.

But he didn't answer. Instead, his eyes began to roll upward under his eyelids.

"Oh my God!" she said again. She had only seen him do this twice before. The first time was when he was an infant and had a flu virus and a fever of about 106. The second time was about three years ago when that same symptom had been followed by a pronounced seizure that had lasted for about three minutes. During those three minutes he had shook violently, and he had bitten his tongue so badly that he had to sip cold liquids through a straw for several days while his tongue healed. And now it was happening again.

A Milestone Day

Jack went into a doubled-up position with his legs pulled tightly up against his belly.

"Jacky, Speak to me!" she almost yelled at him. "Say something, darling. Speak to me."

But Jacky just went limp now, and slid back downward into the water like a limp snake. His mother grabbed onto his hair again, and managed to keep his face above the water. She pulled his head upward and backward, and shoved a washcloth into his mouth to keep him from biting his tongue. Then, just as she feared would happen, he began to shake violently.

He was very difficult to control in the tub like this. Mrs. Green had all she could do to just keep his face above the water and to keep him from fracturing his knees or feet on the sides of the tub. She supported him in this way as well as she could for what seemed like a very long time. Then he just went limp again. He was bluish in color all over his body now, and she realized that he was not out of danger yet.

"Oh no! Honey, snap out of it. I don't want to lose you."

Then she realized that he was choking. She ripped the washcloth out of his mouth, and pulled his mouth open with her other hand. For a moment she couldn't see his tongue anywhere. Then he let out a deep cough, and his tongue came shooting out from the back of his throat. Jacky coughed another deep cough followed by a deep breath. And then his eyes began to attempt to focus again.

"Jacky! Jacky, can you hear me?" she asked desperately.

Jack's color was returning now, and she had pulled him back into a semi-sitting position. He had his hands on the bottom of the tub now, and was beginning to support himself a little bit.

Then he turned his head to look directly at his mother, and asked with a rather bewildered, but well-focused stare, "What happened, Mom? Are you okay, Mom?"

She could see that he was, indeed, okay now. And she also realized that he had no recollection of anything in between now and when he had last asked that same question several minutes ago.

She began to hug him tightly now, and began to cry with deep sobs of relief and motherly love. She held him and just cried for a full minute before Jack regained his composure and strength enough to question her again, "What's going on, Mom? I don't feel burnt anymore. Am I okay? What's going on, Mom?"

His mother was helping him to get to his feet now. "Come on, Jacky. Let's get you out of the tub now. That's enough bathing for today."

Jacky, still puzzled, got out of the tub and allowed her to assist him in drying himself. This was unusual since his mother had left this responsibility to him for the last few years. He saw his torn shirt on the floor, but he just couldn't put it all together. He still felt rather remote and disconnected from reality when he suddenly began to feel very nauseated.

"Mom?" he asked gently.

"Yes?" she returned.

"I feel like I'm going to throw-up."

With that he turned toward the toilet seat, calmly lifted the lid, and just heaved his guts out. Basically, all that came up was bile and chewed banana.

It suddenly hit her. The same thing had happened the last time - three years ago. After his previous seizure, he had become nauseated. He had eaten two bananas that day, too - just about an hour before the seizure. She hadn't associated the nausea with the seizure, but she now remembered having told him on that occasion that he had eaten too many bananas. Their family doctor, with whom they had consulted immediately following the seizure, was unable to arrive at a solid conclusion. Since there were no further occurrences until now, the previous seizure had become reduced to merely a curiosity over the years. But she was now convinced that the bananas were a contributing factor in this repeat occurrence.

Jack took a long nap that afternoon. During his nap his mother checked him every five or ten minutes to be certain that there wasn't a reoccurrence. She had called their family doctor and made an appointment for Jack to be examined the following morning. Jacky had a normal appetite at dinner that night, and the subject of his seizure was never brought up during dinner. However, Mrs. Green had already briefly, but thoroughly, discussed the entire episode with Jack's dad immediately upon his arrival from work late that afternoon. And they talked further that evening after Jack was in bed and his brother had left for an evening date with one of his girlfriends. They knew that they had a very real concern, now that a repeat seizure had occurred. Jack's dad agreed to stay home from work tomorrow in order to drive Jack and his mother to their family doctor's office for this important visit. Jacky slept very peacefully that night.

Now, as he approached the river bank with Cary and Fred, Jack wondered why this particular occurrence had come back into his memory at this time.

5

Cooling Down

As they reached the river bank, Cary began to take off his shoes and socks. All three of them were perspiring fluently, but the air was not nearly as humid as earlier that morning. Jack dropped his boots and just sort of wandered aimlessly into the river still wearing only one sock, and seemingly oblivious to Cary and Fred.

Fred and Cary looked at each other and they could almost see question marks over each others heads.

"Hey, Jacky!" said Cary with concern in his voice. "Are you alright?"

Jack didn't answer, but he did give a faint wave of his hand as he continued into greater depths.

"Hey, Jack," said Fred, "you better slow down. You might hit a drop-off."

Cary had rolled up the legs of his jeans for wading. But now he quickly began to follow Jack into the deeper water, mindless of the fact that he was already in well past the legs of his pants. Jacky stopped at about chest depth, and turned to face Cary. Cary just stopped and looked at Jack. Fred was just entering the water as Jack disappeared under the water.

"Jack!" yelled Cary. And Jack came bobbing up again with a big grin on his face.

"Come on in, guys," said Jacky. "The water's fine."

Cary was both relieved and a little upset, since Jack's self-dunking had caused a shot of adrenaline to surge into Cary's blood stream in momentary panic. But he could see that Jack was okay now, and he began to laugh a little.

"Jeeze!" exclaimed Fred. "For a moment there I thought I was going to have to carry the backpack for the rest of the day; but I see you're back now."

All three of them were laughing now. However, Jack looked pale instead of his usually flushed tone, and his lips were looking strangely blue. He began to shiver a little bit, and his teeth were chattering. Fred and Cary didn't really notice this because they were already too busy trying to dunk each other. The water wasn't really cold at all; but it was refreshingly cool in contrast to this now very hot and cloudless day.

A Milestone Day

Jack began to make his way quickly towards the two of them. Cary and Fred were now so engrossed with their struggle to dunk each other, that they didn't see Jack's approach until it was too late. He caught them both off guard and shoved the two of them off balance. They both went down with a tremendous sploosh!

Jack found this hilarious until he felt a hand grab his ankle. His expression changed dramatically just before he, too, went down - this time, of course, not of his own free will.

"Whoa!" exclaimed Jack just before his wide-eyed expression disappeared below the water line. Underneath the water he could only see faintly. The Mississippi is known to be rather muddy any day, but even more so with the three of them struggling in close proximity to each other.

Jacky found himself sitting on the bottom with one hand wrapped around a large rock and the other hand sinking into a mud hole. This, along with the poor visibility, really spooked him. He began to struggle almost furiously to reach the surface a couple of feet or so above his head. He was on his feet in a few seconds, and took in a huge breath of the warm summer air.

Fred started to push him down again when Cary grabbed Fred's shoulder firmly to stop him. Cary had noticed that Jack still wasn't looking too well right now. Fred looked back over his bare shoulder and saw that Cary wasn't trying to dunk him again. Cary was looking at Jack's face. Fred turned his attention to Jack again, and realized that Jack didn't look like he was enjoying this whole thing as much as they were.

This time it was Fred who asked, "Are you okay, Jack?"

Jack had recovered his composure and stated somewhat unconvincingly, " Yeah, sure! I'm fine now."

"Well you don't look fine, Jacky," said Fred. "You look kinda pale, and your lips are blue, and your eyes are bloodshot."

"That's from the mud," explained Jack. "I opened my eyes under the water. You can't see much of anything down there."

It was obvious that Fred and Cary were not totally convinced; they were both just staring at Jack now.

Jacky looked a little confused. "I'm cold! I'm getting out of here." And he headed for the shore.

Fred pushed Cary down again, and ran for the bank with Cary in hot, but useless pursuit. Both of them were smiling, but not laughing anymore, because Jack had taken some of the fun out of the game. He was sitting on the shore now, and Cary noticed a shiver go through Jack, in spite of the extremely warm temperature. *Maybe just the contrast of the cold and heat,* thought Cary.

Fred and Cary plopped down on the shoreline next to Jacky, and began to soak-up the sun's heat. They figured that in this kind of heat they would be completely dry within the hour, and they were right.

They just sat there for several minutes silently looking out over the river. Then Fred began to get back into his socks and boots.

"What's that?" asked Cary.

"What?" said Fred.

"That thing attached to your boot," answered Cary.

Fred hesitated, and then answered rather casually, "That's a knife sheath."

"But what's that in it?" Cary persisted. "It doesn't look like a knife."

Fred scratched his head and looked around sort of uninterested, but quietly answered, "That's my pick."

"Your what?" asked Jack, who seemed to be turning back to his usual pink, with a little cast of yellow from the muddy Mississippi water.

Fred, sitting bareback with his arms wrapped around his knees, casually turned his head towards Jack and repeated with more affirmation in his voice, "It's an ice pick."

"What do you use it for, Fred?" asked Cary with genuine curiosity.

"I dunno; it just comes in handy," answered Fred. "Besides, it makes for good target practice."

With this statement, Fred withdrew the pick from its sheath, and threw it almost casually at a large tree about twenty-five feet to the left-rear of them. To the surprise of both Jack and Cary, the pick stuck with stunning accuracy dead center in the tree trunk.

"Wow!" exclaimed Jack. "Can I try that?"

"Sure," answered Fred as he got to his feet to retrieve it. But Jacky was already buzzing past him at a run to retrieve the pick.

"Don't bend the point," shouted Fred, as Jack grasped the pick handle to pull it out of the tree trunk.

Jack looked over his shoulder with a grin, and had to give two hard yanks on the handle before the pick was free. Then Jack walked back toward Fred, and asked Fred how to throw it.

Fred took the ice pick from Jack's hand, and said, "You hold it near the point like this," as he demonstrated for Jack's benefit. "Then you sort of throw it straight out, handle first. You don't have to spin it or flip it. It will turn itself around for you."

Jack took the pick back from Fred, took a serious stance, and held the ice pick up and over his right shoulder. He took what he thought was careful aim, and then flung the pick toward the tree trunk. It stuck well off-center with a resonating sound as the handle vibrated.

"See! You flipped it," said Fred. "That's why it vibrated. You don't need to flip it; just throw it straight out toward the tree."

"Why?" asked Jack. "What's the difference? It stuck."

"Yeah, it stuck; but just barely. You'll have a better chance of it sticking if you just don't flip it. Besides, it goes in deeper that way."

"Let me try it, Fred," said Cary.

Cary was fully dressed now, and on his way to the tree to retrieve the ice pick. Cary noticed that it came out of the tree easily this time. He thought he might have understood what Fred was trying to tell Jack. Cary walked back to Jack and Fred's position. Then in one continuous motion, he turned and flung the pick straight away from himself. It stuck with a solid "thunk" this time, but again was well off-center.

"Hey, little buddy!" laughed Fred. "That's pretty good. Have you done this before?"

"Naw, never," replied Cary with a grin. "I've thrown my pocket knife, but never an ice pick. Actually, I think it's easier than sticking a knife - or at least easier than my pocket knife."

"That's probably because your pocket knife is a cheapie, and isn't really balanced for throwing. This baby is front heavy with a light handle," said Fred as he yanked the pick out of the tree trunk. "The handle gives more wind resistance too, so that the blade arc circumnavigates the handle in flight and tends to slow down or pause more when the blade is facing the direction of the throw. That's why you don't need to flip it."

This was exactly correct, but a little too much for Jack and Cary. Cary thought he understood in principle, but he never, ever had heard Fred sound quite so intelligent or authoritative about anything before.

Fred had the ice pick sheathed in a second, and his flared jeans leg fell back into place over the boot and ice pick just as comfortably as if it really was made to go there.

Cary and Jack were both a little awestruck at Fred's detailed analysis, but after a moment's pause they began to gather up their remaining gear. Jack's color looked good now, and they all felt better as a result of their dip in the cool, but muddy Mississippi river. Their jeans were actually already about half dry due to the heat of the day and a little breeze that had begun to blow again a few minutes ago. Jack threw away the remaining sock, and put his second boot on his bare foot.

As they walked up from the river bank toward the ever present railroad tracks, the air smelled fresh, although still heavy with the heat of the day. Fred was carrying Jack's backpack for now. Cary's and Jack's backpacks both had the extra weight of the acquired dry cell batteries. Cary's backpack now had a round, dried, brown stain below where the wounded can of beans had been earlier.

"Gee," said Cary as they reached level ground and crossed the railroad tracks, "it must be nearly a hundred degrees today."

In fact, the temperature had reached a hundred and one degrees. But the current lack of humidity evaporated their sweat almost as fast as it dried their clothing. Their jeans were drying with light brown streaks from the muddy Mississippi water. Actually, they were just a little bit off-color overall. But their sweat was gradually turning their faces back to a normal flesh tone.

They were beginning the first leg of the journey back to the neighborhood. It had been mostly downhill this morning. It would be primarily uphill for the first half of the way back home - in more ways than one!

6
Cary

On the way up from the river Cary began to feel somewhat exhausted, but pleasantly so. Their clothes were still a little damp in places, and the slight breeze tended to keep them cooler than the extreme heat of the day would normally allow. It would be almost all uphill for awhile, and they were moving rather slowly and silently. Cary began to sort of lazily daydream as they slowly progressed the several blocks to Broadway street, which bordered the lower eastern end of O'fallon Park.

He began to think about Sandra Thomasino. She was a classmate of his. She was an Italian girl with a beautiful tan complexion. Sandra had begun to develop a little earlier than most of the other girls in his class. She seemed to like this premature blessing, and tended to flaunt and tease a little. That is to say that she liked to wear light sweaters that accentuated her figure and she liked to solicit attention. She also had an additional physical attribute that was a clincher in attracting crowds of interested boys. She had a natural blue skin tint around her typically Italian brown eyes. This gave them depth and made her very alluring.

The last time that Cary had seen Sandra was almost a month ago. She was sunbathing (perhaps). That is at least what she seemed to be doing in Cary's naive mind. Sandra was sitting (more like posed) on the brick railing bordering her front porch, and supposedly just soaking up rays of sunshine. She was wearing yellow "short-shorts" and a matching tank-top that only came down to the upper ribcage. She was leaning back on her arms with her chin stretched upward to the sun accentuating her flawlessly tanned neck and her arched ribcage. Her legs were outstretched with one knee bent slightly upward. Cary found the "pose" very effective, especially because he was naive enough to think that the pose was natural and with no sexual intent. In fact, he was significantly effected.

Just as he was about to pass her she looked downward and directly at him. This was even more unnerving, but he was able to manage, "H-Hi, Sandy!"

She smiled at him and said, "Hi, Cary."

Somehow he knew that she hoped he would say more. But nothing would come to mind. He was blanked out totally by her seemingly goddess-like appearance at the moment. So the best he could manage after an extensive pause was a quick wave of the hand and a "Well, see you later!" And then he hurried onward. He sensed her disappointment, but she knew that she had gotten his deep momentary interest. In fact, she had made a profound impression on his newly developing hormones, awakening feelings that he had not formerly experienced.

Cary was not a total novice with girls. There was Connie. They were in the third grade - still long before actual puberty - but she was the neatest creation that Cary had ever met. She was a gorgeous little girl with enviable curly blond hair, meticulously well-groomed by her mother each morning. She had been attracted to Cary ever since Cary had shown the sensitivity to protect Georgie (the third grade "sissy") from Derick (the third grade bully).

Georgie was timid and frail. He was naturally referred to as Georgie Pargie. Cary's motivation was purely and simply Georgie's repeated humiliation by Derick. Two important things had been learned from that particular day's protective actions. The class bully wasn't invincible, and he wasn't even a real bully. It was just that no one had ever challenged him before. Once challenged (and defeated for a good cause) he seemed to gracefully accept his lesson. He stopped picking on Georgie, or anyone else for that matter. Also, Cary found that he wasn't the only one who sympathized with Georgie's sensitive plight in life. Georgie was sensitive to the point of needing professional help, but most of his classmates didn't dislike Georgie because Georgie really seemed to like people. He glowed with sensitive happiness most of the time.

Anyway, after that day Connie was sold on Cary as a hero, and Cary was sold on Connie as an angel sent from God. He became her protector as well. He used to walk her home from school and worshipped every minute with her. To put it into somewhat understandable terms for their age - when Connie came into sight or when her attention was on Cary, he sometimes felt like his feet were about a foot off the ground.

Then Cary got sick and missed an entire week of school. When he returned to school Connie was gone - I mean gone forever! Her family had moved away suddenly for a job relocation to another city. This was devastating to Cary, and left a scar that would never heal completely. It was an extreme injustice in life that such a loss could happen to him at such an early age. He was literally heartbroken, almost as if Connie had died and left the world completely. After all, for the size of his world at that time, this is effectively what she had done.

༺ ༻

Cary came to his senses now as he felt Fred rooting through his backpack.

"Hey, Fred! What are you after?" asked Cary.

"Have you still got the picture, Cary?" asked Fred, a little embarrassed at having been caught rooting uninvited into Cary's backpack.

"Jeeze, Fred! How can you have the energy in this heat to even care right now?" asked Cary.

Fred replied, "I just wanted to see if my misfired pellet caused bean juice to spoil your brother's centerfold."

This really seemed to concern Cary. He stopped in his tracks and removed the backpack to search for the centerfold. He and Fred rooted through the backpack, but there was no picture. They searched harder, and started to empty the entire contents onto the pavement when they heard Jack chuckling.

Jack just reached over Fred's shoulder and into his backpack, and extracted the centerfold from his own backpack with the ease of a magician.

"Walla!" he exclaimed to the surprise of Fred and Cary. "I was wondering when you two guys would ever remember this."

They were both still a little puzzled.

"I relieved you of the centerfold when you first discovered the wounded can of beans. See!" exclaimed Jack as he unfolded the page. "It's hardly even stained."

"What do you mean, 'Hardly!'" exclaimed Cary.

"Well, there is a slight brown stain right in the crease," replied Jack.

Cary and Fred examined the picture, and after a long pause, Cary said, "I've had it now. What ever possessed me to bring it along, anyway."

Fred seemed to think that this was a dumb question. But then he was more than a year older, not to mention a little more demented than the average thirteen year old kid. Cary, on the other hand, was only slightly more than curiously interested in such things at this time. To him the centerfold was a curious fact of life that held more than light fascination. But it held little significance in relation to the real world - specifically to such feelings as he had held for Connie or Sandy. Well, on second thought, the centerfold picture may have had more than a little to do with his recollection today of Sandra Thomasino. What he felt when he looked at the picture was similar to what he felt when he was near Sandy. But Sandy was infinitely more real.

"Maybe we can get some stain remover," said Jacky.

"You dummy!" said Fred. "Stain remover is for clothes, or maybe your teeth, but not for a color picture."

Jack just sort of smiled stupidly - and, indeed, his teeth could have used a little stain remover.

7
Heated Situations

They had just reached Broadway street about the time they had stopped to investigate the centerfold situation. All of a sudden they heard the shrill sound of two kids screaming in a combination of fear and excitement. Two bicycles came flying down the last stretch of a very steep, grassy hill in O'fallon Park and continued right out onto Broadway street without even slowing down. The hill, known as Camel's Hump, bottomed out at Broadway street, which could be a very busy street at certain times of the day. But that didn't stop these two free-wheeling dummies.

"Oh, no!" said Cary softly. "It's Bob and Jerry Clintock."

"From the wild bunch," added Fred.

Bob was fourteen now, and a full head taller than Jack and Cary. He was just a little taller than Fred, but much, much denser (both in physical mass and in mental terms). His brother Jerry was

Bob's yes-man, a year younger than his brother, but even denser than his brother (in mental terms). They were the second and third of five really redneck brothers. Currently, in keeping with the idiots that they were, they came screaming out onto Broadway street with no reduction in speed.

"Where's God when you really need him?" asked Cary, raising his palms and his eyes upward. "Couldn't a semi-truck have been coming by just at that moment? Wouldn't it have saved the world a lot of future pain, and unnecessary harassment and humiliation?"

Jack and Fred found this to be very humorous, even though they had each had their own bad experiences with these two under aged Hell's Angels. For awhile they had nothing over their older brother, Tom, who had been the devil himself at times. But Tom was seventeen now and beginning to outgrow some of his evil tendencies. Maybe watching his four younger brothers gave him a reflection of what he had been, or an idea of what he might become if he didn't grow-up a little.

"Uh-oh," said Jack, "I think they see us."

"Crap! Crap!" said Cary twice.

This was unusual repetition coming from Cary. Fred reacted with, "Easy, Cary. Don't get too excited before the storm; there's only two of them this time."

But Cary was remembering how he had managed to bean the oldest brother, Tom, right on the noggin with his metal lunch box with a furious toss from thirty feet away. What an amazing shot! Who would have thought it could hit with such accuracy? Tom must have chased Cary for five blocks before he caught him. Cary still thinks that the only two things that saved his life were Tom's probable fear of Cary's older brother, Sonny, and the fact that he was exhausted by the time that he caught him. Anyway, Tom had a hard head and didn't seem to be seriously injured.

"Here they co'-ome," said Jacky, (with a strange inflection much like "Their Ba'-ack!" from the not yet written movie "Poltergeist").

Sure enough, after a brief pause to survey the three boys from the distance, they were on their way toward the recently soaked, semi-dry trio at high speed.

Cary had forgotten the centerfold for the moment. So had Jack who was still holding it in his right hand as the dynamic duo burned rubber to a screeching stop just inches from the three of them.

Jerry was riding a well used three-speed racer that looked like he had stolen half of the parts from various bikes (and probably had). Bob, on the other hand, was riding a sleek straight-racer. Straight-racers have a no-coast feature on the peddles - the peddles must continue to rotate in ratio to the speed of the rear wheel. He screeched his Schwinn racing bike to a halt via a combination of the rear brake and the force of his well-muscled legs slowing the peddles.

Bob's fierce eyes checked-out the three of them and came to rest on Jack, and the centerfold drooping from Jacky's right hand. Bob's dingy shirt had huge saturated areas under the armpits, and both boys stunk like they had never bathed. Both of the brothers had demented - we're here for trouble - grins on their pocked and pimpled faces.

Bob spoke first, asking, "Whatcha got there, Jacky - a picture of your girlfriend?" Then Bob snatched the centerfold from Jacky's hand. "Well, look at this, Jerry. It's a picture of MY girlfriend, isn't it?"

Jerry snickered as he took a closer look at the picture. Still snickering, he added, "Yup! That looks like her to me. A-yup! it sure do."

"Where'd you get my girlfriend's picture, shrimp?" asked Bob sarcastically. "I can't let you keep this, you know; 'specially since it belongs to me."

Fred was now in a stooped position with ready access to his right boot and the ice pick. Cary saw what Fred was thinking, and simply placed a suppressing hand on Fred's shoulder.

"It's my brother's picture, dodo," said Cary. "And I don't think he'd like to hear what happened to it, either."

"Looks to me like you've already crapped on it or something," said Bob as he held the picture toward Cary and pointed to the pork-n-bean stain. "Either that, or one of you must be chewin' tobacco already." Bob grinned real wide now, and his green teeth protruded like those of a ten year old Mexican jack-ass that had eaten nothing but guacamole and Elmer's glue for the entire decade.

Cary, Jack, and Fred all knew that it was a hopeless situation. Jacky had started to tremble a little bit. He had almost stopped sweating completely in spite of the heat of the day. Fred noticed that Jack didn't look very well, having turned pale again. He stood up, looked sternly and directly at Bob, and then turned to Jacky with concern. But it was Cary who spoke first this time.

"Are you okay, Jack?" asked Cary.

"He looks pale, again," said Fred.

"You mean puny, don't you Fred?" snickered Jerry. "Come on, Bob, let's hit it. These guys are a drag."

And with that Bob gave the three of them a final defiant look, and folded the centerfold down to pocket size.

"Goodbye, girls," said Bob as he tucked the picture into a back blue jeans pocket. "Better get your friend here into some shade before he passes out and wets his pants."

Jack would have been furious as they watched the two of them ride off towards Camel's Hump again. But he didn't have the energy to be furious, so he had to settle for embarrassed and yield to the logic of finding a cooler place to recover.

Cary remembered that there was a small creek that ran through the ravine in the woods in O'fallon Park. If Jack could just manage the climb from Broadway street to the next level area in the park, they would be standing right next to the woods. So they began to walk across the street and up the hill to the wooded area that sat to the north of the notorious Camel's Hump.

Fred and Cary each held onto one of Jack's arms for the climb. There was a slight breeze again now. Fred said, "I think I smell something burning. Do you smell it?"

Cary sniffed the air and just looked puzzled. They were all puffing a little now from the exertion of the hill climb in this heat. Jack didn't react at all to Fred's question, being totally absorbed in making it up the hill. They were almost to the edge of the woods.

Off to their left they could see Jerry and Bob getting ready to make a run down the paved street next to Camel's Hump. Then Bob and Jack were off like two bats out of hell, whooping and screaming as they gained amazing speed on this straight, fast sloping road. Jerry started to pass Bob until Bob took his feet out of the straight-racer peddles. Then the free-wheeling greater momentum of his larger body caused him to pass Jerry quickly.

Cary, Fred, and Jack all watched in amazement as the two brothers screeched to a halt again right in the middle of Broadway street.

"I say again," said Cary with a grin, "Where is God when you need him? Where are all the semi-trucks when you want to see one?"

Fred laughed aloud, and Jack chuckled a little, too. This was a definite sign of encouragement, but he was still pale and barely sweating. Fred and Cary brought their attention back to this pressing matter, and they each took one of Jack's arms as they entered the woods.

A few yards inward the ground began to slope downward toward the small creek. Within seconds they began to pick up a little speed as they worked their way downward. Fred stumbled once, but was determined not to lose his hold on Jack and managed to retain a stable footing. Within two minutes they were there.

"Gads, look how small it's become," said Cary.

The creek usually ranged from about four to eight feet in width, depending on where you approached it. It had shrunk to slightly less than half of its normal size, being about three feet in width at this point with shallows of only a few inches in depth.

Fred bent down and placed one of his hands into the water. "Yeah, but feel how cool it is," said Fred smiling over his shoulder at Cary and Jack. Fred didn't have to say anymore to Jack. Jack just walked right into the middle and sat down.

"O-o-o-h-h-h!" sighed Jack as he sat there shaking from the sudden change in temperature.

Cary joined Jack, but only after removing his shoes and rolling up his pants for wading. "O-o-h-h, wow!" agreed Cary as the cold really bit his feet. "This thing must start underground somewhere; it's so cold."

Fred seemed content to just wash his hands in the creek, and he splashed some of the cold water onto his face and neck and hair. This water was clean; not at all like the muddy Mississippi river. Jack had worked his way to a deep enough spot to sit and soak his muddy jeans all the way up to his waist. But he still looked very pale and was still shaking. Cary noticed that Jack's lips were turning blue. Jack had his eyes closed and his head uplifted as he leaned back onto his arms for support elbow deep in the creek water.

"Hey, Jacky, are you okay?" asked Cary.

After a few seconds pause and no answer from Jack, Fred asked the same question - only a little louder. Jack still didn't answer, but he moaned a little. Cary waded over in front of Jacky, and he noticed that Jack's eyes weren't really quite closed. His eyelids were fluttering between half open and closed, and Cary could only see white where Jack's eyes should be. He knelt down quickly now in front of Jack, disregarding his wet jeans, and lifted one of Jack's eyelids - still nothing but white.

"Fred!" shouted Cary, very frightened now. "Something's wrong with Jack. His eyes are rolling back into his head."

Fred came into the water now, boots and all. "Jeeze, Cary. I've never seen anyone look like this before. What should we do?"

Cary looked confused for a few seconds, and then he saw Jack's mouth droop open. Jack was shaking badly now, but somehow was still supported on his own arms. He began to draw gasping, choking breaths, and Cary was afraid Jack was going to choke on his own tongue. Cary whipped out his half wet handkerchief and wrapped it around two of his fingers. He reached into Jack's mouth and depressed his tongue to open a hole for him to breathe.

"Is he unconscious, Cary?" asked Fred.

"I don't know. I think he's sort of semi-conscious. Let's get him out of the water."

Even with one of them on each side, Jack was a heavy load in his wet jeans. They managed to get Jack seated on the edge of the creek when he doubled up into an almost fetal-like position and began to shake violently.

"Gads!" cried Cary. Cary took the hanky off his two fingers and forced it between Jack's teeth in layers. Fred looked really spooked by Jack's seizure. He thought maybe Jacky was going to die or something.

A muffled "U-u-u-h-h!" came out of Jack's mouth, followed by a "p-h-oo!" as he spit the hanky from his mouth. "O-o-o-h-h," he moaned again, looking around now. "How did I get over here?" His curled-up legs had gone normally slack now, and he tried to regain the greater self-composure of a sitting position.

"We a-helped you over here, Jacky," said Cary as he looked directly at Fred.

Fred returned Cary's look, and read into it that Jack would be a lot better off if they minimized what had happened.

"Yeah, Jack," agreed Fred. "We just kinda helped you over here; you looked a little weak. Are you okay now?"

Jack's color was returning quickly now. He really wasn't sure how severe his attack had been. He wanted to believe that it was nothing like the previous one, which he had gathered from his mother's alarm had been quite severe and frightening. At any rate, Jack felt an acceptance and profound friendship towards Cary and Fred, who obviously had accepted whatever had happened and had taken care of him.

Off in the distance towards Camel's Hump they could still hear the maniacal screams of Jerry and Bob, so they were in no hurry to leave the coolest, most comfortable spot around.

A few minutes later Fred again became aware of the smell of smoke, and commented to Cary.

"Yeah," said Cary, "I smell it too now. It's getting stronger."

All three of them looked upward toward the opposite land-rise on the other side of the creek. And there they could see fairly heavy smoke billowing over the top of the hill and beginning to sweep downward into the creek area.

"What the hell?!" exclaimed Fred. "I think the woods are on fire."

Sure enough, almost as Fred spoke, they could see flames beginning to peak at the top of the hillside. Fortunately, this was in the other direction from which they had descended. Unfortunately, the wind was from the direction of the fire, and the flames were advancing quickly.

"Let's get out of here," cried Jack, "or we're going to be toasted marshmallows before too long."

The three of them took off in a slow run up the hillside. And in a few moments they were standing at the top of the hill and breathing heavily. The heat of the day (and of the fire) hit them again with force. Jacky was sweating normally now.

As they turned around for another look at the oncoming fire, Cary was awestruck at the picture he saw. The sun was three quarters of the way across the cloudless blue sky. However, the smoke had already begun to darken the sun.

Again they heard the screams of the Clintock brothers behind them. Fred turned to face them; they were less than a hundred feet away from them now, and preparing for another run. This time Jerry had ditched his bike at the side of the road, and was climbing onto the handlebars of Bob's straight-racer bike.

"Hey, look at this," said Fred with a laugh. "I think they may be contemplating a suicide run."

"Yeah," said Cary. "Maybe God is watching after all."

"Hey, guys!" shouted Jack. "Our backpacks are still down there."

"Oops!" said Fred.

Cary and Fred were running back down the hillside almost instantly. The smoke was getting thicker, and Fred noticed some furry critters scurrying up the hillside as they descended.

"Gads, Cary!" exclaimed Fred. "I think that last one was a rat."

"Naw, it couldn't have been," answered Cary. "It was too big to be a rat."

"Well lets get the packs and get out of here."

By this time they had reached the creek, and started to retrieve the backpacks. The smoke was enough to take your breath away by now. Their eyes were burning, but they could still see fairly well. Jack was making his way down behind them. He had almost reached them when they turned to run up the hill. They were met by a blood-curdling scream from Jacky.

"A-a-a-h-h-h-h!!" screamed Jack.

"Jeeze, Jack!" said Cary. "What's the matter with you, anyway. We could have had a heart attack."

Jack just pointed to the creek. Scurrying, clawing, and swimming across the small creek were scores of rats of all sizes.

"Oh, God," said Cary as he reached down to pick-up a huge stick to use as a club.

They were across the water in an instant and running directly towards them. Cary swung and hit two of them with a single blow. Jack screamed again, and was already on his way back up the hillside with great speed. Fred stomped his feet to reroute the stampeding hoard enough to reach down to grab his ice pick. Then he, too, began to run up the same hillside as the rats. Cary took advantage of a brief break in the stampede to turn and begin to follow Fred up the hill.

The stampede was upon them again in an instant. *Wow, these little creatures were fast*, thought Cary. He stopped, shouted, and took three more swings with the club, hitting two more of the rats closest to him.

They were almost to the top of the hill, coughing now from the smoke. Then amid stride, one of the smaller rats ran right up

Fred's slightly bell-bottomed pants leg. This time Fred went white, and screamed in shear terror.

"What's the matter, Fred?" asked Cary, himself nearly totally panicked.

Fred didn't answer. He was too absorbed in watching the squiggly hump in his pants leg that had already reached a near dead-end about halfway up his thigh. Then he remembered that he had removed his under pants earlier that day. At that thought he screamed again, and brought the ice pick downward and into his own leg, missing the rat completely on this first swing. Again he raised the ice pick, and this time brought it downward squarely through the rat's body and out the back of his pants leg. He extracted the pick and just stared at the lump in his pants leg for a second. He raised it a third time and started to strike when Cary grabbed Fred's wrist with both of his hands.

"It's dead, Fred," cried Cary. "It's not moving; it's dead."

"Oh, God!" exclaimed Fred - this time almost tearfully; almost prayerfully. "Get it out of my jeans," he cried.

Cary took the ice pick from Fred's hand and ripped a much larger hole in his pants leg starting where the rat had been stabbed. Most of the stampede had passed them by now. The dead rat simply fell off Fred's leg to the ground without a muscle movement.

"Fred," said Cary more calmly now.

"Yes?" asked Fred.

"Fred, you've stabbed yourself in the leg," replied Cary. "B-b-but don't be too alarmed. I think you stabbed yourself before you stabbed the rat."

Fred looked at his leg, and there was one nice neat puncture a few inches away from where the rat had squealed his last squeal. Apparently, the rat had done no damage to Fred. Nor was there the feared puncture mark through the rat. The blade had gone through the rat and out the back of Fred's pants leg. This meant Fred would not have to undergo rabies shots. But he surely could use a tetanus shot.

"Can you walk, Fred?" asked Cary. "Please say you can walk; let's PLEASE get out of here."

Fred groaned as he began to attempt to get back onto his feet. "O-o-h-h!" Then, after a little pause he said, "I think it's more numb than anything."

Cary began to assist him up the hillside. Looking back now, he saw that some airborne remnants of the fire had been blown across the creek and it was still advancing, although more slowly. The wind had suddenly stopped or shifted, so they could breath a little better now. With a little more effort some moments later they were all safely back at the top of the hill.

Cary commented, "Surely someone else has seen the fire by now and called the fire dept."

"Surely!" reinforced Fred, still staring at the wooded area with considerable awe. His leg was not bleeding badly, but a puncture wound seldom does bleed freely. He limped a little as they walked toward the steep paved street next to Camel's Hump.

8

Total Calamity

*J*ERRY WAS CLIMBING ONTO THE handlebars of Bob's straight-racer for another terror run down the paved street towards Broadway Blvd. Bob looked in the direction of the three boys, made something of an obscene gesture, and began another run down the hill.

It was amazing how quickly they gained speed with the weight of the two of them on one bike. About one third of the way down the hill Bob's feet could no longer keep up with the rotation of the straight-racer's pedals. He removed his feet from the peddles, and they gained even more speed immediately propelling them along at an even faster rate. About fifty feet later (a brief time with such momentum, but still too long) Bob made the mistake of trying to re-insert his feet into the straight-racer peddles. He almost succeeded, but then the extreme force of the quickly rotating peddles got ahead of him.

As Bob re-inserted his feet into the peddles the force of the peddles gave a tremendous kick to his left foot, followed by a hard kick to the right foot. The combined immediate effect was that the heavily weighted bike took a DOUBLE skip - from front tire to rear tire and back to the front tire again. Jerry (still riding the "hood-ornament" position on the handlebars) released the handlebars and became airborne. Just before the front tire took the second bounce, Bob applied the front and rear wheel handbrakes. That was the final mistake. When the front wheel impacted the ground for the second time the bike literally bucked Bob right out of the seat. He felt the bike and himself going into a fast forward cartwheel and released his grip on the handlebars. He, too, then became air borne with the bike flying high into the air just behind him.

Jerry had already hit the pavement at about thirty miles per hour. He rolled violently for several yards until he hit the curbing on the right side of the road.

Bob, on the other hand, went straight forward and soon began what seemed to be a non-stop skid on his bare hands and his knees. Although he was traveling slower than Jerry when he left the bike, he must have skidded about twelve to fifteen feet before he stopped. But it wasn't over yet. The bike was still in motion, taking one more tremendous bounce just behind him. And, wouldn't you know it - as Bob rolled over onto his back and looked upward the straight-racer came down right on top of him. He was able to partially deflect the bike with his feet and his bleeding hands, causing the bike to fly off to the right side of the road. The bike, of course, totally missed Jerry who had come to his sudden stop several yards back up the hill where he had hit the curb with considerable force, and rolled onto the grass.

"O-o-o-o-h-h!" moaned Bob. His blue jeans and his knees were badly torn from the pavement, and the palms of his hands were scraped and torn to the bone (literally!). One of his tennis shoes was gone, and the one remaining on his foot had the toe scraped completely through to a partially torn sock.

Fred, Jack, and Cary all looked at each other in amazement. Then they began running down to the area of the accident, with Fred trailing and limping a little behind the other two boys. When they reached Jerry they could see that he wasn't bleeding, except for a bloody nose. He was sitting up, and was conscious, and crying. They quickly passed him on their way to Bob, who was obviously more seriously injured.

As they reached Bob, they could see that he was bleeding badly, and he was obviously in a lot of pain. His hands and knees were bloody- black from the asphalt that had been scraped into the wounds by the pavement. He was definitely a hospital case.

Bob's bike, a few yards down the hill, didn't look much like a bicycle anymore. The frame and the front wheel had been bent severely by the last impact just prior to the bike attempting to land on top of Bob. Also, one of the peddles had been knocked off completely when it hit the curb, never to be found by them.

Just about the time the three boys reached Bob, Cary somehow also managed to notice that a semi-truck came barreling down Broadway at super speed. It flew right past the intersection where Bob and Jerry almost surely would have been if they had completed this run. Even under the circumstances Cary nudged Fred and pointed to the quickly disappearing semi.

Fred chuckled under his breath when Cary commented softly, "The Lord has been merciful today."

Jack was full of excitement as he surveyed the extent of the damage, both to Bob and to his bike. Then he ran back up the hill to Jerry, who was trying to stand up now.

"Are you okay, Jerry?" asked Jack with genuine concern.

"Yeah, I'll be alright. Not that it's anything to you, creep," replied Jerry through his remaining tears.

Jack frowned, and he turned to check-out Bob again. Bob was trying to stand now, but he couldn't get his torso fully erect. He did manage to kind of hobble over to the curb and fell into the grass on his back again. He certainly couldn't afford to fall on what was left of his hands and knees. Fortunately, his face or head had never struck the pavement - a credit to his physical strength and a salvation to his longterm well being.

"O-o-o-h-h-h!" moaned Bob again. His face was racked with pain, and his eyes were welled-up with tears (but he wasn't crying). His expression became rather horrid when he checked-out the damage to his hands and his knees. He was pale, but still functioning. He was a tough cookie - a survivor for certain! He managed to groan out, "Someone had better call my mom to get me home."

"Home, hell, man! You need a doctor - like right now," replied Fred.

Jerry finally made his way down to his brother. "O-o-h-h, Bob! What have you done to yourself?" Then looking at Fred and Cary he said rather shakily, "Someone call an ambulence or something. He's really hurt." This was probably Jerry's most profoundly correct statement during his life to date.

Then Fred remembered his own leg. He wondered how deep the self-inflicted puncture wound had gone. His leg was now beginning to throb horribly with new pain.

Off in the distance they could hear the sound of a siren - or sirens? Apparently, someone had reported the fire.

Within two minutes or so they saw a fire truck tearing along Broadway heading north, followed by another smaller truck in close succession. The first and larger truck stopped where this suddenly disastrous street intersected with Broadway directly below them and the fire. The firemen began to tap the closest fire-hydrant. Almost simultaneously the guys saw a huge extension ladder begin to pivot upwards and swing toward the burning woods. The second truck had passed the intersection, apparently heading for the other side of the woods where the fire must have begun.

A fireman began to climb the already growing (extending) ladder. Even Bob, in his pain, had sat upright to see what was happening.

Bob said, "Hey! Someone go down there and tell them that I'm hurt."

But as the extension ladder gained height, the fireman on the ladder (just riding upward now with a large hose in his hands) was coming closer to their position. It wouldn't be long now before he spotted the unfortunate demented duo and their three adventurous spectators.

"Hey," shouted Jerry.

"He can't hear you yet," replied Cary.

"Gads, Fred!" exclaimed Jerry with his first genuine concern for any of the three of them. "What the hell happened to your leg?"

Fred's ripped jeans leg was obvious enough, but there was also a huge lump beginning to swell and protrude through the ripped area. Fred, too, was becoming increasingly concerned - as well as Cary and Jack.

A fantastic eruption of water began to spray from the elevated fireman's hose. They could also see mist from another spray - apparently coming from the other truck, which was now on the other side of the wooded ravine. The gray/black smoke began to intensify as the battle to "kill" the fire began. Additional sirens were heard in the distance now.

The fireman on the extension ladder was only about two hundred feet from the boys now. Judging from his position and direction, he might be able to see them if they created enough motion. Fred began to wave both arms for attention. The three most mobile boys began to jump up and down while flailing their arms as well.

Sure enough, as hoped, the elevated fireman finally glanced in the direction of the group of boys. He was a rather busy fellow at the time. However, he continued to divert increasing attention to the boys as he was able to do so. He was able to make out that Bob's flailing arms were covered with what appeared to be blood. Then the fireman made some sort of signal to his fellow firemen on the ground, and the force of the water was reduced almost instantly. This gave the elevated fireman the total freedom of one hand. He used this hand to produce a "walkie-talkie," as we would have called it then. The fireman talked quickly and briefly. Then he hung the radio on his belt, and took a moment to point in the direction of the juvenile clan. Now he again directed his full attention back to the diminishing fire, and the water flow quickly rose again to full flow pressure.

Fred began to look very pale now. He looked at his leg again and began to moan. Some very intense pain had begun to return again to his formerly numb leg, and the swelling was now a frighteningly blue, purple bulge that refused to bleed or ooze anything.

Another siren could be heard in the distance. At first it seemed to be fading, but then it began to grow stronger.

Cary looked at Fred, and could see that he wasn't doing well at all. He glanced at Fred's leg and thought, *Boy, is this day going to pieces.* Then Cary did something rare and out of character for him. He walked over to the far curb where the backpacks were thrown, and reached into one of the backpacks. He extracted the pellet pistol.

Cary walked calmly over to Fred, and insisted that he lie down, or at least sit down. He assisted Fred back to the street curbing next to the more severely injured Bobby. Then he whispered into Fred's ear, "Stay stable, Fred. Watch this; it will lift your spirits."

Cary walked over to where he was standing directly over Bob, and withdrew the pistol from his rear jeans pocket. With his back to the elevated fireman, he pointed it right at Bobby's head.

"Okay, thimble-brain! Let's have the picture."

Bobby looked at Cary in disbelief, and managed a surprised "What the hell! What are you going to do with that?"

"I'm going to put a pellet where it will hurt most if you don't relinquish my brother's centerfold." Then he pointed the pistol at one of Bobby's bleeding, bone-bare knees. "You want it in the knees or in the hands? Either way no one will know the difference considering the already extensive damage you've caused yourself."

Bobby looked at his knees and his hands, and then at Cary in total disbelief. Then he began to reach for his rear pocket where he had stashed the centerfold.

"Hold it," said Cary. "Let me get it. I don't want you to stain it with your blood."

O-o-h!, thought Fred, *Icy cold, dude - right on, my man!* Fred was chuckling audibly now, in spite of his injury. His color looked better.

"What are you chuckling about?" asked Bob. And as Cary stooped to remove the centerfold from Bob's pocket, Bobby elbowed him right across the left jaw.

Cary was more surprised than hurt; rather, it was Bobby who cringed in added pain from the impact. Cary extracted the picture and placed it into his rear jeans pocket. He knew that it could never really be returned to his brother's magazine (in it's now stained, slightly bloodied, and multi-folded state). But he thought he might really enjoy telling Sonny the whole story, if it had a significant ending. The centerfold would be a profound souvenir of the events of this day.

Cary then rubbed his cheek where he had been struck by Bob, and smiled at Fred. Then he turned toward Bobby pointing the pistol right at his crotch. The smile left Cary's face, and he looked intent on doing something very grave now.

Bobby cried out as he actually used his bleeding hands to assist in scrambling and scooting his bruised rump (and family jewels) out of the direct line of fire. He knew he was hurt badly. But then again, everything is truly relative to the current situation!

Cary looked serious and didn't hesitate. He began to fire repeatedly, kicking up little puffs of dust between Bobby's legs with each shot getting closer and closer to his implied target.

"Pa-pa-pl-pl-pl-ple-e-e-ease, Cary! Don't do it," cried Bobby. In retrospect, Bob sounded incredibly like Roger Rabbit would sound pleading for a believing ear over thirty years later in the 1990's. He couldn't scoot any further, now cringing in new pain from the badly torn and dirt contaminated palms of his hands which were clasped loosely together in a bleeding, prayer like pose.

"I never really intended to, Bobby," said Cary. "We aren't all animals like you and your brothers. Just remember what I could have done and didn't do. Better yet, think about what my brother might still do. He doesn't have a soft heart about someone messing with what belongs to him....stated possessions including me first. Push me just a little further sometime - just once; just a little bit pl-pl-pl-pl-please!!" mocked Cary.

Bobby was shaking now. Cary started to have a change of heart; some regret for his actions because Bob looked like he was starting to pale - and maybe even go into shock. But the ambulance had just become visible down on Broadway, and would be upon them in seconds now. Bobby had bullied Cary for the last time.

Cary walked over to his backpack and tucked the pistol into the backpack along with the centerfold.

Jacky had just observed this whole scene and was awestruck. He began to loosen-up a little now, and breathed a long sigh of relief. Jerry had gotten to his feet, and was shading his eyes to get a better look at the oncoming ambulance. He wasn't really severely injured. But Cary knew (and was glad) that Jerry would certainly accompany Bob to the hospital rather than stay here alone now - after Cary's very real threat to Bobby's family jewels. Jerry figured Cary didn't necessarily have a particular sibling preference - a Clintock was a Clintock, and Jerry considered himself easy prey without Bob to protect him.

Jerry began to look at the bikes. His was still at the top of the hill; Bob's bike looked totaled. Jerry ran up the hill toward his own bicycle. He retrieved it, and returned to the cluster of juvenile "war veterans" awaiting the approaching ambulance.

Turning to Jack, he asked, "Will you take my bike back with you?"

Jack quickly replied, "Sure!"

Fred would surely accompany the two Clintocks in the ambulance. Fred knew quite well what a severe danger to life and limb a deep puncture wound could be if not treated.

The ambulance stopped briefly at the bottom of the hill, and a fireman pointed to the group's position. Within seconds the ambulance was beside them, and a rear door swung open. An attendant jumped out of the rear, surveyed the situation and turned his attention toward the cab of the vehicle.

"Hey, Danny! Come take a look at this group."

A second attendant (Danny) jumped out of the driver's seat and looked them over quickly. He looked at Bob, then at Fred's leg, and back to Bob again and said, "What in the hell happened to you boys?"

Within a few minutes they had Bob on a stretcher and loaded for transport. Danny and Cary helped Fred to slide into the passenger seat next to the driver. The rear attendant started to swing the door shut when Jerry cried, "Hey, I'm going, too!" He quickly jumped into the rear and the last door swung closed.

They made a wide u turn, and Cary waved sympathetically to Fred as they sped away.

Jacky was still relatively speechless, but his color looked good now.

Cary turned to Jack now and said, "Well, at least we have a ride home now," as he nodded towards Jerry's bicycle.

The two of them smiled and headed across the street to retrieve the two temporarily discarded backpacks.

Jacky said, "Man! I can't believe what you did to Bobby."

Cary glanced momentarily at Jack, then replied softly, "I don't know if I believe it either. I don't think I'd ever do it again." Shaking his head in disbelief, he reached into the backpack once again to assure himself that the safety was engaged on the pellet pistol. Then standing tall again, he added, "Boy, it sure was fun though!"

Jacky gave a stifled nasty chuckle and the matter was closed for now.

9
All Downhill From Here

Cary and Jack passed Bob's lost tennis shoe as they walked up the hill. Cary was walking Jerry's bike until they reached more level ground.

"Should I get Bob's other sneaker?" asked Jack.

"Naw," laughed Cary. "Did you see the one he was still wearing? I don't think they would quite match anymore."

Jack laughed too; then he asked seriously, "Do you think he will be okay?"

"Relative to what? He's certainly going to have some serious scars. He'll be lucky if he hasn't ripped some tendons or permanently destroyed any muscle tissue; not to mention his knees." Cary also thought how fortunate for Bob that he hadn't injured his head or his face - not that his looks were that great (green teeth, acne, etc.). But most of this was correctable with better habits.

Jack and Cary spent a few moments trying to figure out how they could transport two backpacks and themselves on one bike. They finally figured that the best way would be for each of them to wear a backpack. Cary would drive first, and Jack would ride on the frame behind the handlebars. This would be a little cumbersome, but the terrain from here to home would soon be level if they chose the right streets.

And soon they were off, traveling in first and second gear for the most part - only catching third gear on a couple of brief downhill runs. It only took them about ten minutes to be at the northwestern-most corner of Fairgrounds Park, near the lake where Cary had last seen his brother fishing earlier this morning.

They paused for a moment, and Cary said, "Jump off, Jack."

"What's up, Cary?" asked Jacky.

"I think I'll walk from here, Jack. You can bike it around the park and be home in minutes. It's all downhill from here. I think I'll take a walk through the park."

"What for, Cary? You don't think Sonny will still be over here at 4:30 in the afternoon in this heat - do you?"

Cary wasn't sure why; it just seemed like a good idea right now. He was, at least, feeling badly that he had actually fired the pellet pistol so close to Bobby. He looked at the ground and told himself he'd never own a gun. Then he looked back at Jack and smiled.

"Naw, I just want to walk, and think a little. We don't eat 'til about six, so I'll just kill a little time. You'd better get out of the heat; you've had a rough day."

Jack paused for a moment's reflection on a few of the day's events. Then he smiled warmly at Cary and said, "Yes, I guess you're right; I'm bushed. Say, do you want me to take your backpack home with me? Just loop it over the handlebars and it can ride on the front fender."

"Done!" said Cary, more than glad to get rid of the extra weight.

In seconds Jack had tightened the pack straps and was on his way with a quick wave of his hand over his left shoulder. "Hope Fred's alright," he yelled over his shoulder.

"Yeah, hope so!" replied Cary.

Cary waited until Jack was out of yelling range, and then he felt suddenly, but pleasantly alone. It had been a very full day with many new memories. Cary didn't know it, but the day wasn't really quite over yet.

He made his way into the park and towards the lake. This course was the most direct to Clay Avenue on the southwest side of the park. Cary thought he might stop at the dock and soak his tired feet for a few minutes; maybe freshen up a bit at the restroom before he showed his dirty face at home.

As Cary reached the restrooms, he could see only one person on the dock, still about a hundred feet away from him. He started to enter the men's room door when he stopped to take a closer look back toward the dock. *Is it possible*, he thought? .....*I think it is her. Wow! It's Sandra Thomasino on the dock. What's she doing here?.... Dumb question, Cary; it's a free park, isn't it?*

Cary darted into the men's room. He took care of his first necessity, and then rushed to the sink.

"Gads! Look at me," said Cary out loud.

Even in the cracked and dirty restroom mirror he could see that he was a wreck. He began to wash his face and neck vigorously, and ran water through his mud-yellowed hair as well.

"I don't even have a comb," he said again aloud. "Crap!" He ran his fingers through his hair until he saw some semblance of what looked like a normal human being in the mirror. His shirt was still dirty yellow, but at least he looked sort of ruggedly human. A voice inside of him seemed to say, *Well, come on, dummy. She might leave.* Adrenaline and the quick wash-up in excitement in seeing Sandra had sent his pulse and heartbeat racing. So before he left the restroom he looked in the mirror one more time and thought silently, *Calm down; she's only a girl.* And with that he walked boldly outside for his anticipated encounter.

Sandra was still there! Another long, deep breath and he began to walk confidently toward the dock. Sandy was sitting about thirty feet outward on the right side of the dock. She had both feet dangling in the water, and she looked cool and calm looking off toward the distant shore. She was wearing blue jean cut-off shorts and a pink swimming suit top that left a lot of her exposed to the sun. Cary thought that she looked exquisitely tan. As he set foot onto the dock he began to feel himself become nervously excited and physically aroused.

Sandy looked calmly in his direction as she heard his footsteps on the wooden dock. She smiled pleasantly, not seeming the least bit surprised to see Cary. She continued to look at Cary as he approached her, and greeted him with a mellow, "Hi, Cary."

"Hi, Sandra," returned Cary. He was standing almost directly over her now, and although he enjoyed this visual perspective, he felt a little awkward. So he said, "Mind if I sit down?"

Sandra replied smiling, "Of course not, silly," and patted the dock right next to her.

Cary nervously but gladly complied. He sat down about a foot from her with his knees pulled up against him, rather than dangle his shoe-clad feet in the water.

Should I ask the obvious? thought Cary to himself. "What are you doing here, Sandra? Are you here by yourself?"

At first she just looked at him, and Cary thought, *Dumb opening!* But then she smiled again and scooted almost right up against him. Still smiling, and almost face-to-face now she pointed across the water to her little brother playing alongside of the bank about fifty yards away. Cary followed her gesture to spot the boy.

"I'm baby-sitting," said Sandy, "Or little brother sitting, actually."

Cary could feel her breath on his cheek as she spoke directly at him. He turned his attention back to her and there they were face-to-face, eye-to-eye with no more than six inches between them - those beautiful deep brown eyes with the bluish skin-tint around them. He could smell her breath as she spoke.

"Want some gum?" she asked.

She smells sweet, thought Cary - a mixture of her sweet breath and a hint of perfume actually accentuated by her own natural smell in the now diminishing heat of this nearly spent day.

Cary had paused a little too long before he replied, "U-h-h, yes. Thank you," as he opened his mouth and took the gum which she had already unwrapped, and was placing slowly and personally into his accepting mouth. If Cary were a fish in the lake smelling the bait, he would surely be hooked by now. And he was hooked - at least for now - hook, line, and sinker as they say.

"Ouch!" they both heard from the direction of Sandra's brother, and this broke the magic.

"What's the matter?" yelled Sandra. "Are you okay?"

"Yeah!" returned little five year old Tommy. "I lost my stick in the water and got my foot wet," said Tommy while rubbing his knee.

Earlier Sandra might have gotten up to go and investigate more thoroughly, but not right now. She immediately turned her attention back to Cary who was still looking at Tommy.

As Cary spoke he turned his attention back to Sandra. "He seems to be a-a-l-l-r-r-ight," he managed, now again looking directly into her deep eyes. She knew he was well-hooked now. He knew it, too!

"Is it okay to call you Sandy, u-u-h-h, S-Sandra?" asked Cary with a little stutter.

"Sure it is, Cary. That's what my family calls me all the time - just like Thomas is little Tommy."

Cary wanted to kiss her. They were so close; she looked and smelled so sweet. He really didn't know what to do with this moment in time.

"Where have you been today, Cary?" asked Sandy. "You look like you've, uh, been on some kind of adventure or something."

Cary came to his senses a little now, realizing that by now he must look (and perhaps smell) like he had just arrived from a different world. Actually, for all her composure, Sandy was quite taken by

Cary too. He seemed to her to be sort of rugged and sexy. And now, because of her gum, somewhat sweet-smelling as well.

"Oh! Uh, we've been down to the river - Jack and Fred and me. I-I guess I'm a sight by now," replied Cary finally.

"Oh no; you look fine. I mean you look, uh, rugged; like you've had a full day of fun," smiled Sandy. She was still talking right at him, and only a few inches away by now.

Cary couldn't take it any more. She had to be "coming on" to him. Not even his mother treated him this well or spoke to him this sweetly. He reached out and place his right hand around the back of her neck and pulled her into him, and they kissed. His was a gentle kiss at first. But Sandy seemed to know where to go with it from there. Cary was about to release her when he felt her hand on the back of his neck encouraging him to continue.

"Whatcha doin'?" asked a calm, little voice behind them.

They broke clean and looked up in surprise. Tommy had somehow magically appeared behind them - or so it seemed. Cary thought, *Boy, time (and little kids) really can fly when you're having fun.*

Sandra spoke up with, "We were sharing our gum, Tommy."

"Sure," said Tommy smiling. He paused, still smiling, and said, "I'm gonna tell Dad."

It was just about then that Cary realized that Sandy still had her hand on his neck. He felt her fingernails dig into his neck in reaction to Tommy's statement. Still unaware of Cary's wide-eyed reaction to her nails, she now released Cary and got up to chase little Tommy down the dock.

Cary sat there in a dazed mixture of pleasure and amazement as he rubbed his neck and watched Sandy chase after Tommy. Then he got to his feet and joined them on the bank. Sandy was threatening Tommy at first. But she ended up bribing him with the rest of her gum, and promising more "brotherly love" to be forthcoming in the near future if he would keep his little mouth shut. Somehow Cary got the idea that Sandy and Tommy had been through this scene before.

A car drove up to the curb on Sarah street a couple of hundred yards away. There was a beep from the horn, as Sandra and Tommy quickly and abruptly settled negotiations. Then Sandra complied with a wave to the vehicle.

Sandy looked at Cary with sad eyes for the first time ever, and said, "That's my Mom. She's back from shopping now, and we've got to go."

Tommy was already trying to pull her in that direction, but she resisted long enough to reach a hand out toward Cary. He did the same, and they just managed to brush fingertips before Tommy gave Sandy a sudden jerk. Then they were off at a run toward the vehicle.

Sandy looked over her shoulder, obviously wanting to say something more (call me? see you at school?). But nothing came out, and they were gone in a moment.

Cary stood there for at least three full minutes. He watched the car disappear, had a million thoughts and feelings, and then a cool breeze began to bring him back to reality.

"W-o-w!" sighed Cary. "I think I'm in love."

He knew he didn't really mean this literally, although at the moment that is exactly how he felt. Cary had kissed girls before. But it really didn't count for anything except curiosity or playfulness. But this was entirely different. The feelings produced here were likely to have a significant effect on his attitude towards all girls and upon his life in general.

Well, now that the ground had come back up to meet his feet (or visa-versa), he decided to be on his way home. The remainder of the distance to his home only took about ten minutes. However, within that ten minutes Cary had another million thoughts. He would have to do a little maturing just to handle the thoughts and feelings of this day. He gradually managed to place them into a vaguely sane perspective.

As he walked through the screen door into the kitchen his mother glanced up from her cooking and said, "Well hello, stranger." Then she gave him a double-take, and eyed him up and down thoroughly. "Looks like you had a pretty full day, Hon. Everything okay?"

Cary knew that he would eventually have a little explaining to do in reference to Fred's injury, and the fire, and little things like that. But for now he chose to just say, "Yeah, fine, Mom. I think I'll clean up for dinner."

"H-m-m, good idea," she replied.

10
Dream Sharing

Cary lay in the tub just soaking and thinking, just coming back down to earth and reality. He mused that time must fade in and out in one's memory. For whatever reasons, he could not remember when he had begun to develop the recent pubic hairs that now floated on the moving surface of the water. At the same time, he was too tired to care about such a seemingly insignificant detail.

Well, he thought to himself finally, *so you've had a new level of experiences today. So let's sort them out and file them for future reference.*

This was, of course, exactly the right thing to do, when the mind has had more input than it can readily digest. It was best to sort and file a few things away right now during the time period that he had available to him.

Let's see now, thought Cary. *We have seen the dangerously dynamic pimpled duo become hospitalized - yeah! Or should that be "great!"? And well deserved! Yes?....Yes!,* thought Cary. He had made a judgment, but one that he felt was necessary for self-preservation, and as correct as it could be for right now. *They got what they deserved; some punishment for their miscalculated adventures - some payment for dumb things done! Enough for that one; what about Jacky? And Fred?*

What Cary had to first block-out right now were the emotionally stronger feelings or impressions left by his encounter with Sandra Thomasino. These feelings were important - very important, indeed. However, some training within him had already taught him to place those things first that were associated with long-term friendships, or longer-term situations of any kind. Then the more recent things, along with their emotional predominance, could be handled with greater tact and understanding. Cary knew that the day had been an accumulative MIND BLOWING sequence of events. He knew that he had to arrive at tonight's supper table not only physically clean and refreshed. He needed a total perspective that would allow a smooth progression of thoughts and ANSWERS to today's events.

He knew, somehow, that he would be - not on trial - but certainly an object of many questions. His brother would be full of questions. And his mom and dad only knew that he and Jacky and Fred had planned an adventurous trip to the riverfront. He also knew that he would at least have to justify the granting of this privilege. It was surely a borderline call for his parents to let Cary pursue this rather distant adventure. They saw him as a son whom they had loved as a most cherished possession for almost 13 years now. He had never been this far from home without adult supervision more than once or twice in his life (and never with permission).

With the soothing warmth of the water, Cary's mind started to fade a little - to drift on a pleasant sea of thoughts and feelings. He was drifting between reality and that twilight zone just before sleep claims the conscious mind. There was just a brief period of time in which imaginative thoughts (near dream-state) took on some semblance of reality. For maybe a few brief seconds (or minutes?) Sandra appeared to be right there in the bathroom with Cary. She was wearing the same cut-off shorts and pink swimming suit top that Cary saw her wearing earlier today.

"Hi, Sandy," said Cary (in his drowsy mind).

Sandra splashed the water toward Cary. Strangely, he didn't feel the water strike him. Rather, as dream progressions tend to flow, she was upon him before the impact of the water could be noted. She was kneeling in the tub with one leg on each side of Cary's legs. Her clothes were wet now, and she reached forward and put her forearms around Cary's neck. She started to kiss him when the next thought in Cary's mind was, *Is she really here?* This was quickly followed by a shocking total awareness that he was, indeed, now awake and in the tub quite alone.

"Cary," came his mother's voice from a distance. "You've got ten minutes 'til we eat, Honey." There was a silent pause. "Did you hear me, Cary?"

With reluctant submission to reality, Cary answered twice - first in an inaudible voice; then more loudly, "Thanks, Mom! I'll be there."

He could hear his dad exchanging small-talk with his mother. There was no audible indication that Sonny had arrived home yet. Cary began to climb out of the tub. In a candid moment of self-indulgence he turned back toward the tub, and reached out his right hand.

"May I assist you out of the tub, and back into my mind?" asked Cary of the imagined Sandra. In his imagination she accepted his hand, and her small, somewhat immature breasts shook as she jumped into an imaginary towel.

This fantasy completed, Cary turned to open the bathroom door and hesitated for just a moment. He continued onward when he felt secure that Sandra was well re-implanted into his permanent memory for all that she had given him (both in reality and in his imagination).

He opened the door and proceeded into his (and Sonny's) bedroom with a towel wrapped loosely around his slender, tanned waistline. It would only be himself and Sonny, along with mom and dad, at the supper table tonight. Their sister was staying at a friend's house for a couple of nights. This was one less person to evade if the questions got to be too intense.

Ten minutes to supper time, thought Cary. *Got to move faster. Had Sandra by coincidence really been thinking or dreaming of me as well? Was it a dream?,* he wondered. *It seemed so real for at least a few moments. Wow! What a fascinating thought!*

∞

Sandra sat quietly at the supper table with her mom and her little brother, Tommy. They could here their dad humming an Italian melody in the bathroom, while he washed his hands for the evening meal.

Sandra glanced at Tommy, and Tommy mockingly made puckering kiss/ kiss motions with his lips. Sandy raised one hand slightly above the table-top and clenched it into a fist to warn her "loving" brother of their agreement. Tommy then mockingly batted his eyes "lovingly" in recognition of the extorted rewards he knew Sandra would yield to seal his rat-fink mouth.

She began to review the day's events and emotions while they waited patiently for Dad to arrive at the dinner table. She hadn't bathed before dinner. But she had taken a brief, and somehow very pleasantly refreshing nap. Although she didn't remember any dreams, she did somehow feel an intense closeness to Cary that was unexplainable - but, again, very pleasant. Whatever the cause, life is often reshaped around feelings. *Yes!,* Sandra thought, *I must pursue him. I must know more about him.*

Unfortunately, reality took command as Sandra's dad's Italian belly entered the kitchen, followed closely behind by the rest of his body. Their mother quickly set the last bowl onto the table and sat down.

In keeping with his very Italian and very Catholic background, once seated, Sandra's dad's first words were a prayer. He began with, "Let us pray. Bless us, O Lord, and these thy gifts ......"

Sandra was still thinking, *Yes, I want to know this boy much better.*

11
The Truth Comes Out

Cary had been in bed for almost an hour now, and he was just now beginning to wind down - to feel settled. After dinner, Cary had told Sonny almost everything, including almost shooting off Bobby's family jewels. Sonny loved that part. He wasn't even upset when Cary showed him the bean-stained souvenir of the day's events. But eventually, after many questions, the final comment by Cary's brother was, "If Dad and Mom knew about the centerfold and where it came from, you'd be a dead brother." Sonny then finally drifted off to sleep. That was at least twenty minutes ago. Cary was just now beginning to fade, having reviewed the dinner conversation in his mind over and over again.

ಆ

Dinner had proceeded almost routinely until they had just begun to take the dishes from the table. Yes, there had been some questions pertaining to the day's events. Had Sonny made any fantastic catches that day? Did anything exciting happen on Cary's outing? etc.

Both Sonny and Cary answered the relatively routine questions with naturally routine answers. Sonny knew enough about Cary and his real world to know that there was more to tell. He'd catch a significant glance from Cary, or a nervous reaction or such between answers. He easily gathered that Cary wasn't telling the whole truth and nothing but the truth. Cary knew that Sonny knew, too.

Then, just as they began clearing the dishes, the telephone rang.

"Who would be calling right at supper time?" asked Cary's mother as she walked to the phone. Telephone calls were not as common then as they were to become in later years.

"Hello!"

There was a pause followed by, "Oh? Oh, really!" Cary's mother gave him a very serious look. "Is he still in the hospital? Oh?.... Oh, he came home with whom?....The Clintocks? What were they doing there?........N-o-o-o! Really?" Another serious glance at Cary - the kind of glance that sort of stings when you receive it.

Cary looked really nervous now, and Sonny was all ears. Cary's dad, usually slow to be angered or aroused, began to look intense as well.

"Oh, My!" she continued. "And they let him go home like that? Oh, my!" She rolled her eyes back into her head in disbelief, followed by another more serious look at Cary - if looks could kill!

"Yes, Ellie. Yes, I think that would be a very good idea."

Jacky's mother, thought Cary. *She's spilling all the beans on today's events. Did Jacky talk? Did someone call her?*

By now Cary's dad was leaving his chair with many invisible (but obvious) question marks poised above his head. "What's happened? What's going on?" he asked.

She just put a reassuring hand on his shoulder, and then held up her hand to retain him for another moment. "Yes, Ellie, I'll be over about nine am....yes...uh-huh, sounds good. Yes, I can hardly wait to get an update. See you then, and thanks, Ellie....Goodbye for now." She still stood there with the phone to her ear - click!

Cary's mother slowly set the telephone handset onto the telephone base, still recovering.

"Well, what the hell is going on?" asked Cary's dad. He seemed a little shaken as if he was expecting the worst.

"Oh......it's nothing to worry about. Thank God everyone is alright - or at least at home healing."

"Healing?" asked Cary's dad. "What happened? Some kinda' accident or something?"

"I think maybe you had better ask YOUR SON. Apparently a lot more happened today than he has told us"....long silent pause; hard questioning stares; question marks over Dad's and Sonny's heads, etc.....

"Well?" she finally asked. "What did happen today, young man?"

All eyes were on Cary now. Sonny was smiling with enthusiastic anticipation. Mom was building a little dark cloud over her head now, along with the question marks that both her and dad were still sporting.

Cary just sort of gave in and sighed. "You may want to get some coffee. I'd hoped to avoid all this; it's going to take awhile to tell you everything that happened."

Sonny was intensely glued to his chair now. Dad and Mom just kind of slowly slid back into their sitting positions, obviously all ears. Cary was a little relieved now. At least they didn't look like they were going to attack him anymore. They could see that Cary was obviously alright, so they began to look less severe, although intensely interested.

Cary cleared his throat, and began - shakily at first. "W-w-ell everything began very nicely.... Right, Sonny? I mean, when you saw us everything was okay! Right?"

"Well of course; sure!" said Sonny, obviously not eager to be dragged into this one. "But it was still very early. You guys weren't even dirty yet. Come on, Cary! Tell us what happened today."

Cary paused and then he began again. "Well, everything was really fine for the early part of the day, or at least until well after Fred shot the first rat."

"Shot a rat!.. With what?" asked his now wide-eyed mother.

"W-w-with his pellet pistol, Mom. You know how he is."

"No, how is he?" she asked sharply.

"Now settle down, Margaret, and let the boy tell his story," said Dad.

Thanks, Dad, thought Cary, and he began again. "Really everything was okay I guess 'til the limb broke....or maybe even until the Clintock brothers arrived later."

Mom had locked-jaws by now. Cary had obviously (in his nervousness) hit on a couple more things than Jacky's mom had related over the telephone. Cary didn't know how much she knew, so he sighed again and began again. "I guess you really want to know about Jacky's fall first."

His mother's eyes got even bigger. "Jacky fell?"

Oh, boy! thought Cary. *I'm really blowing this one.* He glanced at Sonny who was really trying hard to stifle his laughter.

"Well, he didn't exactly just fall; the limb broke that he was climbing out onto. Jacky was lucky though; the mud at the bottom saved him from serious injury..."

His dad quickly interrupted with, "How far did he fall?

Cary hesitated a moment, swallowed hard, and answered, "About thirty-five feet or so."

"Oh my dear Lord!" exclaimed his mother. "What was he doing that high up in a tree?"

"Well he wasn't really, mom. He was only about ten feet up. But he was also a good eight or ten feet out past the edge of the river bluff, which added another twenty-five feet down to the river bank."

Cary's mom looked just a little faint as she visualized this statement. Cary's dad, patted her and squeezed her shoulder. "Easy now, Momma. Let Cary tell us the story. Obviously Jacky is alright or Ellie would have said something."

"Yeah, he's fine, Mom. Like I said, the mud softened his fall. The tough part was getting Jacky out of the mud."

Sonny was almost in a seizure himself by now, trying to suppress what could be disastrous laughter at this serious moment in time. He had to get up from the table and go to the bathroom. No one but Cary seemed to detect the muffled laughter in the distance (from the bathroom). Sonny flushed the toilet about three times to gain sound cover (and his composure) before he returned several minutes later. He was smiling, but controlled now.

And so it went. They must have questioned Cary for over an hour while he continued to explain on and on. Just a few of the question highlights and responses included things like:

"Bobby snatched what out of Jacky's hand?" asked Sonny. There were many raised eyebrows over this one. And on and on it went:

"He carries an ice pick in his boot?" asked Cary's mom.

"Gads, bro', how many rats came out of there?"

"Fred really stabbed himself?"

"Did anyone wrap Bobby's hands?" asked dad.

"Was his bike really totaled?" asked Sonny. "Awesome!"

"How many fire trucks did you say?"

"And one ambulance! Any police?"

And finally from his dad, after they had all calmed down considerably, "Well, Son. What do you do for an encore after a day like today?"

Cary sort of smiled sheepishly and looked at the table. "Nothing dangerous for awhile, Dad."

"Well, you've got that right," replied his dad. "Maybe nothing at all for awhile would be more appropriate."

Cary looked pleadingly at his dad for a second, and then back down at the table. He knew that if he looked penitent, he probably wasn't in as much trouble as he had feared. In retrospect later, he was proud that he never had to tell them about Jack's seizure. Currently he had to suppress a smile from the corner of his mouth when he thought of the final significant event in the park with Sandy. *Wow!!*, he thought excitedly. *I've got to know her better.*

In brief retrospect, Cary knew he'd had one heck of a day - to put it mildly.

As Cary lay in bed his eyes were finally becoming heavy. *I sure hope Fred's okay*, he thought sincerely. *I wonder if Bobby had any brain damage? Naw....not possible! NOT!!* Then, *O-o-h-h, S-S-Sandy!!....* was his final thought. ....z-z-z-z-z-z-z-z-z-z.

At the same instant in time, Sandra was already beginning to dream about Cary. Her little brother Tommy was already dreaming about spearing a huge fish.

Cary would sleep very soundly at first, and rest more peacefully towards morning. To his conscious recollection, his mind was nearly dream-free for most of the night. At least this is the way it seemed since he had been very, very tired after this adventuresome and satisfying day. In reality, he did have many dreams, some of which involved Sandra with in-depth emotion. He thought he remembered dreaming about Sandra, but the memory of this dream-state was more of colors and unusually deep emotions than of real experiences.

He awoke, feeling rested and fully refreshed the next morning. He had slept in his underwear, as he often did. But this morning his t-shirt was unusually saturated with perspiration when he awoke, and his underpants felt strangely sticky. He had a profound feeling that something in him had changed, although he didn't know exactly what. He knew for certain that he wanted to feel fresher and cleaner. Cary went immediately to the bathroom, first out of necessity. But then he spent several minutes refreshing his sweaty body with a damp washrag, damp wiping himself overall before dressing himself.

Cary would spend a lot of time during the next few days before the first day of school rather preoccupied with Sandra. He didn't really quite understand why, but he felt good about it. He had, in fact, unknowingly experienced a new level in physical maturity last night. Things would never, ever be quite the same again.

Sandra awoke refreshed, too. However, her first nearly conscious thoughts confirmed that somehow she was even more intent on pursuing her newly discovered interest in Cary.

Sonny hadn't gone fishing this morning. He was still sleeping peacefully (if you could interpret his heavy snoring as peaceful).

Cary would not see much of Fred or Jack again until well after the first day of school. Nor would he see Sandra at all until the first school day (they were to be in the same class). Cary thought that perhaps he will have forgotten his preoccupation with her by then. But would Sandra allow this line of thought to continue as Cary might have preferred? I tend to doubt it.

There were many other friends (and some enemies) in this early pre-teen year and the teenage years that followed. But enough for now! Perhaps more later.

The End, For Now